**Carter placed a charge
between the two generators ...**

He had one ball of C4 left and he intended
to use it on the ventilators or the entrance
doors at the surface. As he started to rise
from his crouched position, he heard the
bark of an AK-47 from behind.

The slugs hit him in the kidneys and the
rib cage, and finally a glancing shot to the
side of his head. They were like hammer
blows in the hands of a powerful man.
They threw him against the wall in front of
him.

He slowly felt the lights go out ...

NICK CARTER IS IT!

FROM THE NICK CARTER
KILLMASTER SERIES

PRESSURE POINT

KILL MASTER

NICK CARTER

JOVE BOOKS, NEW YORK

KILLMASTER #230: PRESSURE POINT

A Jove Book/published by arrangement with
The Condé Nast Publications, Inc.

PRINTING HISTORY
Jove edition/October 1987

ISBN: 0-515-09168-5

Jove Books are published by The Berkley Publishing Group,
200 Madison Avenue, New York, New York 10016.
The name "JOVE" and the "J" logo
are trademarks belonging to Jove Publications, Inc.

PRINTED IN THE UNITED STATES OF AMERICA

10 9 8 7 6 5 4 3 2 1

Dedicated to the men of the
Secret Services of the
United States of America

PROLOGUE

Coming in off the North Sea, bouncing off the balding mounds of rock the local Scots called mountains, then striking at the stunted trees and sparse growth, the harsh winds buffeted the ancient walls of the inn at Poolewe.

It was past seven. The inn, its rooms empty at this time of year, played host to the locals in the common room as it did every night. It was a small room, seating no more than thirty with perhaps six more at the bar. The walls were stucco, smoke-stained, dotted here and there with old carriage lamps, most of them not working. The ceiling beams were at least a foot square, had been cut by hand, trimmed by the ancients, and looked as if they'd been put in place shortly after His busy six days of the Creation.

The dozen seated men were a surly bunch. Living on the barren hills of northern Scotland, tending stinking sheep, constantly pinching pennies had made them taciturn, as their fathers had been. They sat in small groups, drinking their pints slowly, holding the chipped mugs in gnarled hands. They talked softly and ignored the stranger who sat at a table alone as he had for a week past.

A tall man in his mid-forties, well muscled, with a face that looked as hard as the stone of the mountains outside, sat alone and smoked an old briar pipe. He didn't approach them, knowing that any attempt at striking up a conversation would be futile. He was dressed as they were, in a worn tweed coat, a wool sweater, green twill work pants, and heavy boots. Unlike the others, his boots were not streaked with sheep droppings, nor were his hands scarred from shearing. He was a stranger, and in the harsh land that was the northern coast, strangers sat alone.

Geoff Hood had been in Poolewe for more than a week. He stayed in a bed and breakfast place run by an elderly woman, and he walked the coast morning and night. Sometimes he rode a bicycle down the single-lane roads to nearby villages, Gruinard, Aultbea, and Ullapool. Sometimes he sat in the pubs there, as much alone as he'd been in Poolewe. The locals knew his every move, reported from wife to wife through the Highlands grapevine, but they left him alone.

He understood them keeping to themselves. His people had lived not far from here at Dingwall. They had died when he was small and he'd been sent off to an aunt in America. Northern Scots were clannish, even within their own communities. It seemed the farther north one went, the closer knit they were and the less friendly.

He walked from his scarred old wood table to the bar and had his pint filled. The owner spoke only when necessary. He filled the stranger's mug and took his money, then turned away to run a rag over wood kegs of port and sherry, seldom used.

Hood had returned to his table, a man of infinite patience, when the door banged open and a man entered. He was a younger version of the others, but unlike them he wore a broad smile on his face. The others muttered about the draft from the door but failed to greet him, going back to their muted conversations.

The newcomer was short, about five feet. He was almost as broad without being fat. His face was weathered, his clothes abused from days of hard work without the benefit of soap. He had an aroma all his own, but his personality made up for it. He greeted the owner with a laugh and a bellow, accepted a filled mug and looked around the dimly lit room.

The powerfully built man wandered slowly to Hood's table. "Damn me if it's not a stranger we have," he said, the Scottish Highlands lilt rolling off his tongue.

Hood grinned. He motioned for the man to sit. "Geoff Hood," he said, holding out his hand.

"A Hood, no less," the young man said, taking the proffered hand in a callused one. "Most Hoods I've known came from Glasgow. Accounts for your city hands," he went on in a loud voice. "Name's Jock Fraser."

The others turned to scowl, then went back to their talk, shaking their heads.

"A city boy, but originally from Dingwall. Been in America," Hood said, using the reference to the United States all Scots used. "Been there since I was a kid."

"America. The more luck to you," Fraser said, a broad smile revealing only stumps of teeth at close range. "I been down to London for a few years, and to Liverpool. Ship's plater. No work like that now."

"So it's back to the sheep?" Hood asked.

"Back to the sheep shit, the cold waters of the lochs, and the colder hearts of the old men," he said with a laugh.

"A man's got to eat," Hood said, starting out slowly, not wanting to spook his man now that he finally had someone to talk with.

"So what in hell you come to Poolewe for? End of the bloody earth, this place." Fraser's mug was empty already, and he wiped his mouth with a grimy back of his sleeve.

Hood moved to the bar for another round, answering over his shoulder as he set down the empty mugs.

"Been sick," he lied. "Came back to look at the old home."

"Yessir. They do that. I've seen more than one. Scared sick by the devil and scooted back to the home place," Fraser hooted, louder than ever, if possible.

"The devil seems to have followed me. Almost afraid to walk the cliffs," Hood said, getting a first reference to the recent tragedies into the conversation, letting the thought dangle.

The rumble of conversation stopped in the room. It was quiet for a few seconds until Fraser spoke. "The devil, is it? We don't rightly know. Why don't you get out of here if you don't need to stay?" he asked, the smile sliding from his face, leaving it looking ordinary, as surly as the others.

Hood smiled. "I didn't mean to open up a bad memory. Let's drop it. I'm not really afraid. Probably a coincidence."

A rumble of disagreement rolled around the room, though no man looked at the stranger.

"Don't be too damned sure. Bad around Gruinard Bay. There was the boy," one of the old men joined in.

"And Old Alf," another of the old men said, his voice sad from the loss.

"Who's Alf?" Hood asked.

"Constable. Been here since before I was born," Fraser said, his uncertainty dissipating.

"He disappeared like the boy?" Hood asked, handling them with kid gloves. "What happened to them?"

"Don't know. Found his bike at the cliffs. Up at Gruinard Bay. West shore it was," he said, almost draining his pint. "It wasn't like Old Alf. He'd report in every time he came to a telephone." It was always Old Alf when they talked of him, never just Alf.

"Took his job very serious, he did," one of the old men said, turning his chair partway around.

"He could have fallen," Hood offered. "The boy could have slipped."

"The lad may have been daft, but he was like a bloody goat. He'd nae fall, mister. My cousin's boy, he was," one of the men croaked, his voice like a cracked board.

"Well," Hood said slowly, "I'd say it was just coincidence. I know it sounds strange, but they were probably both accidents."

"Something's going on here we dinna ken," Fraser muttered, speaking for them all. "Strangers been seen skulking along the cliffs. Then two people disappear. No coincidence, say I."

The others grunted assent.

Hood had learned all he was about to from these men. He smiled, now that he seemed to be accepted. "I understand all Americans are supposed to be rich," he said. "What say I pretend I'm rich and buy you all a pint?"

The owner came to life and started to fill the mugs as if he were afraid the stranger would change his mind. Chairs scraped as some turned to drink to Hood's health. The American raised his own mug to them in a toast and suddenly felt fear.

While the craggy faces looked at him and smiled tentatively, he felt fear as if the devil had, indeed, caught up with him. He'd worked for AXE, a highly secret intelligence agency, most of his adult life and he'd never had the feeling. A minor cog in a large network, he'd heard veterans of the intelligence community talk of the feeling, but he'd never experienced it.

Mainly because it signaled the end. And the end for someone like him wasn't retirement. The end was a visit from a skeletal figure in a hooded, flowing robe leaning on a scythe.

A couple of hours later, the American left them with regrets. They had told him to come back the next night. It had been the first sign of hospitality in a week. Jock Fraser had bought him a round in the end, and he left feeling bloated, about two pints beyond his limit.

His bike was in the rack outside the door. It was covered with a fine mist from the waves that broke against the cliffs behind the inn and sent a fine spray across the village when the sea was running high.

The constable, Old Alf, had been lost at Gruinard Bay. That was what they'd said. The AXE agent debated the wisdom of making the journey at night, but something, some feeling of a meeting with destiny, drove him on.

He'd have to pedal along the narrow road to Aultbea, almost five miles, then cut across the rocky slopes to the cliffs and the bay.

Inland, on the strip of asphalt, marked every hundred yards with a layby, a waiting spot to let others pass, he felt totally alone. Men were at their pubs where they belonged. Women sat at home by themselves or in pairs sewing and talking. The lone man smelled peat smoke from some of the cozy hearth fires as he passed along in the dark. The lighted windows providing a dim glow were far apart.

A full moon was up there somewhere, but thin clouds kept its helpful glow from finding the narrow road. The batteries had long since died in the rusted flashlight on the bicycle he'd borrowed from his landlady. Dust-smeared reflectors were still hanging on the front and back, but they were almost useless. Why would he need them anyway? He was alone. He could have been on the moon and he would have felt no more alone.

Geoff Hood passed through Aultbea with only the bark of a dog signaling his presence. It was an old dog, or one with a sore throat. He wasn't even permitted the bark of a healthy beast to break the silence of the journey. It could have been the bark of a dog's ghost, it had been so soulful and weak.

A fine mist attacked him about a mile out of town. The bay was to his left across the fields and rocks.

He walked his bike. He would have left it, but he thought he might return a different way. The distance to the cliffs was a lot longer than he thought. He fell twice and skinned both hands.

Soon the sound of breaking surf told him he was getting closer. The spray was like a fine rain. It soaked into his clothes and wet his wind-blown hair.

He was at the edge of the cliff before he realized a vast emptiness loomed in front of him. He leaned the bike against an outcropping of rock and pulled his pipe from his pocket. It was still dry and half full from his last smoke at the pub.

He scratched a wooden match against the matchbox and lit the pipe, protecting the flame against the wind.

His last smoke, he thought suddenly. It sounded like the prelude to an execution. He had become morbid tonight. It was not like him.

Without warning, the moon came out. It was full and yellow, casting a bright and cheerful light on everything he could see.

The bay was huge, about five miles across. Whitecaps were turned to silver by the moon as it cut a sparkling swath through the water. Damned if it didn't look like a picture postcard, he thought.

Light flashed off something to his right and deep below the cliffs . . . a reflection.

He saw it again . . . something reflecting like the glass of a telescope.

But what would a telescope be doing down there?

He strained to see. The head and shoulders of a man far below were illuminated by the moon. The dark head bent to the right and the flash of a reflection could be seen again.

What the hell was he doing there? Hood asked himself. He had just told himself the answer when he saw a stab of orange flame and something punched him in the chest . . . hard.

He held his chest, blood coursing through his fingers. As he fell forward, he could feel air rushing through his hair.

The last thing he remembered was the beauty of the water, the feel of his own blood, the smell of salt air, and the crack of a rifle.

ONE

Nick Carter reached for his cigarettes on the night table, trying not to awaken the woman beside him. He flipped one of this custom-blended cigarettes from their elegant case, flamed it with his gold Dunhill, and inhaled deeply, blowing smoke to the ceiling.

He lay naked on the bed, his tall, well-built frame tanned to perfection. His brown eyes, bronzed body, and black hair were in sharp contrast to the whiteness of the sheets. The jarring note to this image of relaxed masculinity was the collection of scars; his body was a pattern of knife slashes and puckered bullet wounds. Some old wounds showed up white and shining against the darkened skin.

Carter had just completed an assignment in Saudi Arabia for AXE, a supersecret intelligence organization working out of Washington. In that Middle Eastern kingdom, he'd baked his powerful body in the sun, lying on the white sands of the Arabian Gulf shore. It had been part of an assignment to seduce a KGB agent and protect the royal family from assassination.

The job had gone well. Given a few days of R and R by David Hawk, AXE's hard-bitten chief, he'd chosen to spend them with Cynthia Talbot of the AXE station in London. He'd worked with her several times, and they enjoyed each other's company. Their relationship was comfortable, neither making demands on the other.

He thought about the night before, the perfection of Cynthia's body and the urgency of her responses. He never doubted that a stop in London on the way home would soothe his nerves, the exact opposite of his assignment. Seducing KGB sirens, while they kept deadly weapons close at hand and with guards patroling nearby, was somewhat less than totally pleasurable.

The telephone rang. It sounded twice, quickly, in the British fashion. He picked it up before it could sound again. Cynthia stirred but didn't wake up.

"Yes?" he said softly.

"I thought I'd find you there," a raspy voice said with a chuckle.

David Hawk was Carter's boss, the man who had created and had always headed AXE. The agency's headquarters were at Dupont Circle in Washington under the cover of Amalgamated Press and Wire Services.

Carter could visualize the older man sitting in his office—the shock of white hair, the lined features, and the inevitable foul-smelling cigar clamped between his teeth. He was a veteran of intelligence work since he'd helped form the OSS in World War II, one of the best of the breed. They had worked together for more years than Carter cared to recall. In the process, they had come to respect each other. They had developed a relationship more like father and son than boss and employee, unspoken except when alone in times of great stress.

"You know me too well," Carter replied. "And I know you. Something's cooking or you wouldn't call."

Cynthia stirred and raised herself on one elbow so she could hear who had telephoned.

"You remember Geoff Hood?" Hawk said.

"I worked with him a couple of times. Why?" Carter asked, knowing the answer. It was always the same answer in their game.

"I sent him to Scotland on what looked like a routine investigation. He's disappeared. I think he's dead," the commanding voice of the man in Washington said.

"What was he investigating?" Carter asked.

"Two locals disappeared in the past month, one a constable."

Carter stubbed out his cigarette in the ashtray, trying to think of a reason why AXE would be involved in such a routine case. "Sounds like something that would be handled by Scotland Yard," he said.

"The local constabulary have been blocking the move. It's probably a matter of pride," Hawk said. "They don't have to take Scotland Yard's help unless ordered to by the home secretary."

Carter could hear him drag on the cigar and could imagine the acrid smell of the top-floor office on Dupont Circle. He looked at his Rolex. It was three in the morning in Washington. Sometimes he believed the old man never slept.

"We have been called in because the prime minister wanted to keep her MI5 and MI6 people out of it."

Carter was intrigued. "Why the hell would she do that?" he asked. "It's got to be a lot more important than it sounds."

"Inside information. The area of the disappearances is on the northeast coast facing the Hebrides. A huge anchorage at Gruinard Bay. Used to be a refueling station for the British fleet during the Second World War," Hawk explained in his rapid-fire delivery. "Abandoned now. But the prime minister received a tip saying that all the land around there had been bought up secretly. It encompasses all the caverns where bunker oil used to be stored in underground tanks." He paused for a moment to add emphasis. "We think this could be big. Very big."

"I'm not so sure . . . I still don't see it. Unless the land's been bought up by a consortium she can't trace . . . . What's she afraid of? Another cabinet scandal?"

"That could be it. If it is, she's got to keep her people out of it. *And* the British press," Hawk added vehemently. "The worst damned scandalmongers in the world."

Carter knew his boss sometimes had a blind spot when it came to the press. "She asked the president for help," Hawk went on. "He couldn't send in his usual spooks, so he gave it to me. It could be important or it could be nothing. That's why I sent in Hood. Now that he's disappeared like the others, I want you to find out why we lost an agent."

"Do you want me to start today?"

"Yes. Let me know what the hell's going on," Hawk said. "And, Nick, keep it low-key if you can. It sounds political to me; I'm almost sure of it. We find out and get out quickly. Unless you run into something big. Then you report to me."

After Hawk had hung up, Carter lit a second cigarette and sat back against the headboard, thinking. Hawk had not said it all. No one killed an AXE agent without suffering the same fate if anyone in the secret agency could manage it. The designation N3 and Killmaster made Carter an official dealer of death when circumstances demanded. If he found who killed Hood, he or she was dead.

Cynthia, a tall woman, dark like Carter, reached

across him, her breasts brushing against his chest, and took one of his cigarettes. She looked at the tiny gold NC next to the filter and smiled indulgently as she lighted it. "I can ask for a few days off and come with you."

"No."

"We could be a tourist couple exploring the unspoiled Scottish Highlands. It's a good cover."

"No, thanks. I'll go in quietly and alone. It looks like small potatoes. If it turns out to be something big, I may need help from the London office."

He slipped from the bed and glided to the bathroom where he quickly showered and shaved, then returned to the bedroom. Carter reached for his socks and underwear, pulled them on, and put on his shirt. Before he put on his pants he taped a small gas bomb, about the size of a large walnut, high on his inner thigh. Sometimes the bomb, affectionately called Pierre, was filled with a gas that stunned. More often, the gas was lethal.

When he'd pulled on his pants and slipped into his shoes, he reached for the soft leather harness that housed Wilhelmina, the 9mm Luger that had saved his skin on many a tough assignment. When the gun was in place, he strapped a chamois sheath on his right forearm and slipped in a second faithful companion: Hugo, his razor-sharp stiletto.

He always felt better when he was armed. He had no reason to believe he couldn't carry the weapons safely in the United Kingdom. Taking his private arsenal on commercial flights usually required some advance planning, but Carter had already decided to rent a fast car and drive all the way to northern Scotland without using public transportation.

Cynthia had dressed while he armed himself. She seemed to read his thoughts. "I've got contacts for getting a car. You want a beat-up one with speed, right?"

"Exactly. An old Rover 3500 will do. The more beat up the better, so long as it sings on the highways."

Carter took the superhighway M1 all the way to Leeds in the Midlands before stopping for lunch. He had a pint of Whitbread's and a sandwich in a pub just off the highway before refueling the Rover and starting up again.

He cut across to the Lake District, took A74 out of Carlisle, and reached Glasgow in time for a late tea. The highways were not crowded and the patrols had not bothered him. As often happened in Europe, he averaged a respectable eighty miles an hour, and enjoyed every minute. The question was whether to go on and reach Poolewe at dark or start out early in the morning.

He took a room at an inn north of Glasgow at a village called Palloch, and spent the evening at the pub room sipping strong English brew.

He managed to talk to a few of the locals and a couple of tourists. He questioned them all subtly. No one knew anything about strange activity just north of Loch Marie in Scotland. Apparently the local constabulary up there was not bothered by news hounds.

Early the next morning, Carter sat with the innkeeper, had a bowl of porridge, and was on the road at seven. The driving was not as fast as on the highways of England. He recognized many historical names as he drove: Glencoe, Fort William, and Fort Augustus. He saw the towering majesty of Ben Nevis, the black and forbidding waters of Loch Ness, and finally, tired and hungry, pulled up at a hotel in Inverness for lunch.

Again, he questioned carefully. Half the patrons were Americans working on North Sea oil projects. They were more news-conscious than the Scots but had heard nothing of the disappearances even though they lived and worked a scant fifty miles from Poolewe.

It was a bright, sunny day as he left Inverness and drove, with less urgency, up A832 to Gairloch and finally Poolewe. The village was on the sea, surrounded by rounded hills of bleak rock. The lower part of the village was settled around the Ewe River that ran from Loch Marie to Loch Ewe and finally out to sea. Poolewe was made up mostly of small houses. Unlike the thatched roofs of England, these were covered with slate to withstand the harsh sea breezes. The upper part of the village was made up of a few salt-bleached wooden houses on the craggy rock coast above Loch Ewe. It was quiet. The one public house he could see was not busy. Few people were on the roads.

Carter drove the few streets of the village before stopping at an attractive cottage, one of the many displaying the sign Bed and Breakfast. It was close to the River Ewe and an easy walk to the local tavern.

Carter dropped his bag in his room and set out for the pub he'd seen as he drove in. He sat at the same table where Geoff Hood had sat and was accorded the same welcome. He waited patiently, not bothering the locals at first, eating a hot meat pie with his ale and listening.

Finally, as he sat, long after his sparse supper, he heard snatches of conversation from the other tables that he'd been waiting for: they were talking about Hood.

The tall, hard-looking American, dressed in brown slacks and a brown herringbone wool jacket, picked up his mug, dragged a chair across the dusty floor, and moved to one of the occupied tables.

The four men sat, startled. The owner started to move from behind the bar, then thought better of it.

"I'm a friend of Geoff Hood's—you know, the American who disappeared," he said. The four men sat silently, dour and suspicious. "I've come to find out what happened to him."

Carter wasn't like Geoff Hood or the few tourists who visited the pub. He was more like the landowners whose orders were to be obeyed, or the retired army colonel who lived in town. His eyes held them as if commanding an answer. They all knew their usual attitudes wouldn't work with this one.

"Stood us a round or two just before he left, he did," the oldest of the locals said. He was a small man, his mouth caved in around his few remaining teeth, his eyes mischievous as he eyed the newcomer and his own empty mug.

Carter turned briefly to the owner. "A round for everyone." Then he turned back, looked each man in the eye, deliberately, slowly. "Now, tell me what you know," he said.

A stony silence followed before one of them spoke. "He sat and talked to Jock Fraser, he did," a dour old sheep man said. "Asked questions about the wee lad and Old Alf."

"Who are they?" Carter asked as the owner placed five filled mugs on the table, froth welling and spilling around each one.

"Disappeared like your friend," another of the men said. "Old Alf was a constable who bicycled through every day. Come up from Gairloch, he would, and stop in to look around."

"And he disappeared?" Carter asked.

"First it was the boy," an old man, his hands twisted by arthritis, said as he raised his mug to his lips and drank. "At first we thought the lad had wandered off. Strange he was. Not all there, so to speak," he concluded, a light foam settling on his tobacco-stained mustache.

"Then a few days later Old Alf's bicycle was found at the cliff's edge and *he* was gone," the first old man said. "Your friend's bicycle was not a hundred yards from where they found Old Alf's."

"Where was that?" Carter asked.

The owner had come up to stand behind them. "West side of Gruinard Bay," he said, joining in. "You drive to Aultbea, then a couple of miles further on you have to park and walk toward the cliffs. A couple of miles out of town was where the bicycles were found. Right at the top of the cliffs."

It was no mystery that he would suggest driving, Carter thought. The beat-up old Rover stood outside, the only car he'd seen for miles. "What about the local police?" he asked. "What are they doing?"

"You might ask the sergeant at Gruinard. He covers the whole coast up to Lochniver," the owner said. "Stubborn man, that. He's about to find the answers hisself or no one will. Damned fool!"

"You some kind of police, then?" the oldest one asked, his breath enough to kill the heather that blew on nearby hills.

"No," Carter replied. "Just a friend. A good friend." He drained his mug and stood to leave. "I've had a long drive from London. I'll see you all tomorrow," he said as he turned to the door.

•   •   •

In the Rover it took him only minutes to drive to Aultbea and through to the north end of the village. He found an old cart track a mile past the last house and drove inland until he was out of sight of the road next to a deserted barn.

He opened the car's trunk and unzipped a small gym bag. In minutes he had changed into black fatigues and transferred his weapons. He put a small but powerful pair of field glasses in one of the pockets of the fatigues. He also took a small leather case the size of a cigarette pack from his bag and shoved it in one pocket. It was a packet of syringes and drugs devised by Howard Schmidt at AXE headquarters. The information specialist sometimes came up with gear that Carter found very handy.

Standing by the car in the moonless night, Carter was almost invisible. He stopped to listen. He could hear the sound of breakers crashing against rock. Instead of walking to the edge of the cliffs, he returned to the road and walked away from town, examining the side of the asphalt for signs. The shoulder of the road was bare earth, flat and free from gravel.

He passed several laybys without finding what he was looking for. He saw plenty of signs that sheep had passed by—hoofprints and tufts of wool—but no sign of man.

Half a mile further on, he found a set of tire tracks in the earth. They had been made following a rain and had been washed flat by later rains. No mistake. Bicycle tires, old and almost bald from years of wear.

Carter didn't stop long to examine them, but kept up his search. It was after ten. The pub would be closing. Someone might come along at any time.

A hundred yards along, he found a second set of

prints, fainter than the first. Perhaps they had been made earlier, or the ground had not been as soft at the time. It didn't matter.

He started tracking from the road. The trail led to the cliffs. Every twenty feet or so, Carter found another imprint that kept him on a direct path for the cliffside. As he moved toward the sea, the smell of salt air grew stronger. Finally, after twenty minutes of careful tracking, using his penlight as infrequently as possible, he came to the cliff. This was where either Geoff or Old Alf spent his last few minutes on earth.

All through the search, Carter's brain had been working on a second problem. How had the men disappeared? Had they been carried away or had they pitched forward to fall onto the rocks below? If they'd been shot from the sea, the velocity of the slugs would have knocked them on their backs. Even if struck from an angle, they might have fallen backward.

He searched carefully for sets of footprints. Only those of the constable or Geoff were apparent. He had seen the prints of only one man as he'd followed the bicycle tracks, and the ones he'd found at the cliffside were the same.

So no one had attacked the men here and thrown them over.

He moved to his belly so he wouldn't be seen as a silhouette if anyone was below or out at sea. The moon had come out just at the wrong time. Taking the glasses from a pocket, he focused on the rock face near the sea. Only from an extreme angle could a marksman hit a body at the cliffside and have it fall over the edge.

To his left, the cliffs stretched toward the west entrance to Gruinard Bay. He saw nothing on the rock face.

The bay itself was a huge expanse of water. He could imagine a part of the British fleet more than forty years ago, a mighty armada, formed up to take on fuel and leave to do battle with the enemy. Again, he saw nothing suspicious.

To his right, the moon brightened the upper cliffs but left mostly shadow at the base of the rocks. At the waterline, far to his right, he could see a cave entrance of some kind, narrow, almost indiscernible.

Carefully he panned along the base of the rocks. His glasses were rubber-covered with deep shields around the lenses to prevent reflection. He held each lens cupped in one hand to add to the effect of the shields. In no way did he want moonlight to reflect to someone below.

Someone below. It seemed to be the only answer. If someone had bought up all the land, including the caverns, would they be using them? If so, what for?

Carter intended to go down and find out. But first he wanted all the intelligence he could get. He would keep up his vigil until he learned something.

Suddenly, light reflected off glass. It was only a momentary thing, but it was unnatural—man-made.

Carter zeroed in on the source. Now the moon's light was dulled by low clouds that had scudded in from the sea. But he could see something . . . a human form . . . a man with a gun.

The reflected light had been from a scope.

So he'd been right. A rifleman was down there. Why? What the hell did they have to hide? he wondered. And who the hell were they?

It was Carter's job to find out.

TWO

It was well past midnight. The winds had picked up. The temperature had dropped ten degrees. In the black fatigues, with minimum clothing underneath, Carter was cold and uncomfortable.

He had crawled down the rock face a foot at a time. It had taken the best part of an hour. The rock had torn his hands. The chalky deposits of seabirds had attacked his nose and smeared the black cloth.

He had stopped to check on the sentry a few times with the glasses. The man's image grew more distinct. He was tall and looked strong. He was dressed in an olive green uniform with a crest of some kind on one shoulder.

As he got closer, Carter had some luck. The guard was relieved by a smaller man. It would have helped to know how long between shift changes. No matter. This man had just come on duty. Carter figured it would be at least four hours before anyone checked on him. Long enough.

He was within a hundred feet. The last part would be the most dangerous. He couldn't carry his gun or knife in either hand. He needed both for crawling.

Slowly he closed the gap, aware of the scraping of his fatigues against the rock. The sound wasn't carried to the sentry. The crashing of waves against rock drowned out any noise.

When he was about fifty feet away, Carter saw that the man carried a sniper rifle over one shoulder instead of the submachine gun he expected. The man alternated between sitting, his back against the cliff, and pacing the shelf of rock that was his station.

He was like sentries the world over. He was bored and uncomfortable. He undoubtedly wished he was anywhere but there. His mental attitude was probably the same as his fellows. Why here? What the hell was there to see? A stupid, worthless job.

The man's state of mind made Carter's job easier. Almost too easy. After more than an hour of crawling and the concern for his vulnerable position, when he finally crept up behind the man and delivered a karate chop to his neck, it was an anticlimax.

He was wrong. The small man was like a hard rubber ball. The blow that would have floored most men left him unaffected. He swung the rifle stock-first at Carter and missed by inches. The wood shattered against the rock face. Again, the noise was absorbed by the pounding of surf against rock.

They stood facing each other like fighting cocks. Carter had his weapons, but he needed the man whole and ready to talk; the capture would have to be hand-to-hand.

The rock slab was probably fifty feet by twenty. Next to it, an opening in the cliff's face loomed black and menacing. Carter would have to explore it later, but first he had to subdue this small tiger.

The man in the olive uniform tried a blow with his left foot that would have been devastating if Carter hadn't ducked. In turn, as he bent under the blow, he delivered a chop to the man's ribs and heard bone splinter.

Pain creasing his face, the smaller man, extraordinarily strong for his size, tried a blow with his right foot. The result was the same. Carter countered and delivered another slam to the body. The sentry now had cracked ribs on both sides of his chest and he hadn't touched his taller opponent.

Carter was concerned that the struggle was going on too long. Someone might come out of the cavern at any moment. Even above the sound of the waves, the noise of the fight might carry to the interior. He moved under the next charge, swung around, and grasped the smaller man in a choke hold. He held it for twenty seconds until the guard's full weight pressed against him.

Carter let him drop. Time was against him. He pulled the leather case from his pocket and fumbled with its clasp with cold hands.

It held a half-dozen color-coded syringes, and Carter had been well trained in their use. The two yellow ones were harmless: a few drops would put his prisoner out for an hour—all he needed. The two green syringes were for interrogation. They could elicit the truth to all questions or fry a brain beyond redemption, depending on the dosage. The red syringes were lethal, causing a bloodless, silent, quick death.

He took out a yellow syringe, purged it of air, and stuck it in the guard's neck.

It had taken all his strength, but Carter had carried the unconscious sentry the way he had come, a few feet at a time, to the deserted barn where he'd parked his car. The crumbling cement of a foundation stood nearby. Charred pieces of wood nestled among the weeds, almost indistinguishable as bits of a house that had burned and been deserted. Local rumor persisted that it had been occupied by a one-legged sailor and his family almost forty years earlier.

Carter eased the body onto a pile of old straw in the barn and placed the small leather case nearby. He tied the sentry's hands and feet to rotting partition walls and slapped him awake.

"What the hell . . . ?" the man mumbled in Russian. The accent was from one of the southern republics of the Soviet Union, possibly Georgia.

"What is your name?" Carter asked in the same language, but in cultured Russian, the language of Muscovites used by most of the KGB.

"Who are you? Why am I tied? Where is this place?" the man asked, fear evident in his eyes.

"I will ask the questions," Carter said, his face looking as if it were cut from stone, his voice like the crack of a whip.

"You can go to hell! I don't talk to KGB, or CIA, or MI6, or whatever you are."

Carter reached for a green syringe, squeezed out the air at the top, and let a few drops squirt out. "This will make you talk. But it could also fry your brain," he added. "It's up to you. Talk and we don't need it."

"Is that sulfazine?" the man croaked, his face white.

"No, I'm not one of the animals from the Serbsky Institute. That's for your KGB bastards. But this drug can be almost as bad," Carter said, aware of the shortage of time. If those below missed their man, they would probably come out of their holes looking for him, whoever they might be.

"Screw you. I'm not giving you anything for nothing," the small man said.

"As I said, it's up to you," Carter said, pushing the

needle into a prominent vein and pushing the plunger. The sentry's eyes rolled up into his head as the potent drug coursed through his bloodstream. It took only a few seconds for the drug to reach his brain.

The Russian screamed and pulled at his bonds, then was still, breathing hard, his chest rising and falling in a regular if rapid cadence.

"What is your name?" Carter asked. He didn't really care, but he wanted his answers to start with small truths and work up to big ones.

The answer came out with reluctance. The sentry was still fighting the drug. Carter expected it but knew that the small man's resistance would subside soon.

"Alexei Alexandrovich Borodansk." It came out slowly, the voice uncertain—slurred.

"Are you a soldier?" An obvious question, but part of the technique.

"Yes."

"What are you assigned to now?" Carter asked, keeping the questions simple.

"Guard duty."

The answers were short, but Carter expected that. He was satisfied. He had to do it this way. But he was hurrying it. It was a race against time.

"What do you guard?" he asked.

"The pens. The entrance."

"Pens for what?" Carter asked, afraid he had already guessed the answer.

"Submarines."

The answer Carter dreaded came slowly from the guard's lips. The Russian was still now. Relaxed.

"Are they nuclear-powered?"

"Yes."

"How many warheads can they fire?"

"Five."

"Describe the missiles. Are they nuclear?"

"I'm only . . . a guard. I think . . . think so. Why would they . . . not be nuclear? All nuclear." The answers were disjointed, the words slurred.

Carter knew he would have to stay away from technical details with this one. He absorbed the information and could guess the rest. Miniature subs. The old storage tanks had been cut out and disposed of. Submarine pens had been built. Did the Russians think they could operate a base under the noses of the British? It sounded unbelievable, but the facts spoke for themselves. They had got away with it up to now.

He forced himself to stick to the questioning and not speculate. "How many subs are here?" he asked.

"Twenty."

"Are they all operative?"

"Nearly all. A couple are in dry dock inside."

"How many can the caverns hold?" Carter asked.

"Don't know. More."

Carter didn't want to break the pattern. He didn't want any "don't know" answers, so he switched the topic.

"Who bought the land?" he asked.

"British guy . . . powerful . . . member of their Politburo or something," the guard said. Carter was almost sure his prisoner didn't know much about the people behind it, but he tried a few more questions.

"What's his name?"

"They call him . . . the Squire."

"Is there anything special about the subs except their size?" Carter asked.

"I think so . . . heard one of the men . . . the ones in

white coats . . . saying they couldn't . . . couldn't be detected."

"Like a stealth plane?"

"I don't . . . I'm . . . what is that?"

"A plane that radar can't find."

"Yes . . . something like that." The voice was disjointed. The guard didn't look well. His face was pale, almost green in the dim light. "They said it . . . wasn't . . . wasn't perfect yet . . . but they . . . were almost . . . something . . . invisible . . . couldn't be seen under the water."

Suddenly his breathing became shallow and his chest no longer rose and fell as it had. Carter felt his pulse. It was weak—very ragged and irregular.

Carter put his ear to the man's mouth. No sound. No breathing. No pulse.

He cursed softly. Sometimes the drug had peculiar side effects, but he'd never seen anything like this. He put the drugs away, untied the man, and carried him to the cliff. As he tossed him over, he thought about Geoff Hood, Old Alf, and the young boy. He didn't like to kill that way, but maybe it helped even the score a little.

Back at the car, Carter pulled a small but powerful radio from his case and called AXE's London office. The agents there were supposed to monitor his frequency twenty-four hours a day. In minutes he was patched into AXE's computer control circuits and was put through to Hawk immediately.

"Hello, N3. Find out anything interesting up there? What happened to Hood?"

Carter told his boss about the guard, the submarines, and the Englishman who was a member of Parliament.

"I want a check on the syndicate that bought this place," he said. "I also want to know why the prime minister suspected it was one of her party members," he added. "How did she find out? No one up here notified Scotland Yard."

"I'll check," Hawk said. "It looks like we were right. This *is* something big. We've got to stick with it."

Suddenly flickering lights appeared in the darkness. Flashlights.

"I've got to go. I see men at the edge of the cliff," Carter explained.

"Take care, N3. Keep me posted," the older man said.

The soldiers below had obviously missed the guard and were looking for him up on the rocks. They were still about a half mile from him.

Carter didn't try to hide the evidence of his presence in the barn. But he did pull out some dried brush and eliminated the 3500's tire marks after he'd backed the car to the asphalt. They'd know he was the stranger in town, but he didn't want to make it easy for them.

Carter drove the battered old car down to the small cottage where he'd taken a room. He'd registered in a hurry, giving the owner, Mary Wyness, money to ensure she didn't rent the other rooms while he was there. Then he'd left for the pub.

He vaguely remembered her. She'd been washed-out, middle-aged, nondescript—a carbon copy of thousands of poor, tired widows the world over. He hadn't even allowed her time to give him a key when he'd rushed in and taken a room. Damn! She'd undoubtedly locked up and gone to bed hours ago.

But Carter saw a light in the front window as he

pulled up. The door was open. Mary Wyness met him at the door. She was wearing a bright red robe and had brushed out her hair. It was streaked with gray, but was shiny and framed her face. Her glasses rested on an open book, and Carter found himself admiring a pair of large hazel eyes. This was quite a change from the mousy creature he'd met earlier. She was no beauty, but she'd taken off a good ten years.

"I thought you'd like a drink and some company," she said.

"Actually, I'm exhausted," Carter said. "Planned to hit the sack right away."

" 'Hit the sack.' I haven't heard that expression for years."

He suddenly realized she wasn't a local. She was a transplanted American. "I think I will take that drink," he said, now curious about her.

"Good. I know why you paid me not to rent my other rooms. You don't want anyone else around." She poured out what looked like gin. "You're here about the ones that are missing, aren't you?" She raised her glass. "Here's to you," she said. Carter guessed it wasn't her first of the night.

"What makes you think that?" he asked, sipping his drink.

"You know—you marry a Scot, come here to live. Think you're settled for life. He was a prosperous farmer." Her voice was vague and far away. "He died after a couple of years and I found out he'd mortgaged to the roof." She drained her drink and poured another. "So, I took what was left and bought this place —started to go to seed. Should have bought a one-way ticket to the States." She gave a short, harsh laugh.

"Answer my question," Carter said evenly.

Mary Wyness looked at him over her glass for a few seconds. "My first husband told me he was in the diplomatic corps," she finally said. "We went on several foreign assignments." She turned her eyes away. "He lied. Turned out to be CIA. Recruited me to do a lot of his legwork—the safe part. He was shot and left in an alley five years ago." She brought her eyes back to his. "You remind me of him," she said slowly. "You're one of them, aren't you?"

Carter said nothing.

"First the boy. Then Old Alf. Then a stranger disappeared—one they're trying to keep quiet. Probably one of yours," she said, leaning over with the bottle and refilling his glass.

Carter took a swig. Whatever the stuff was, it was potent.

"What do you mean, 'keep quiet'?" he asked.

"I don't trust Sergeant Penny. He's in charge of the local constabulary. Why not call in Scotland Yard? No disgrace. The locals say he's too proud." She paused to take a sip from her glass. "I think he's being paid off," she said.

She was more than a little drunk, and Carter wanted a few more answers now, before she was too far gone.

"What happened to the boy?" he asked. "Any theories?"

"Someone bought up all the land around the bay. All of it. Put up a new fence around the bunkers. The boy was a bit off, you know? Liked to climb things. Not much to climb here—trees too stunted—no other fences. Too much of a temptation for the kid."

"So?" he asked.

"So someone didn't want him on the other side of the fence."

"Tell me about the bunkers," he said.

"Huge cement bunkers. Stood unused for years. Roads leading down to the caverns. New air vents and fans installed. Rusted-out elevators been cleaned and serviced. All fenced in now."

"Any activity inside the new fence?"

"Strange activity," she said. "Seems sneaky to me. A convoy of trucks loaded to the hilt once a week or so. It's as if someone's trying to keep a low profile while doing one hell of a lot of work."

"Noise of work going on down below?" he asked.

"Too much wave action from the sea. Hides everything else."

"And Old Alf? What about him?"

"Alf was a good cop. Better than they deserved here. He turned this place upside down looking for the kid. He got too close," she said. "I think someone threw him over the cliff."

"That simple?"

"Maybe," she said. "I've thought about it. Looked at all the possibilities. That's what I think."

Carter was impressed. The training with her husband had stuck. She was probably very close to the truth. "Why not tell the sergeant?" he asked.

"Told you," she slurred, swallowing the rest of her drink. "He could be on the wrong side."

She was refilling her glass as Carter turned tiredly toward his room. The night was full of surprises, he mused.

THREE

Everything was new and strange to the young boy who crouched against the submarine's bulkhead, his eyes wide with wonder. The control room was crowded with sailors, their uniforms spotless white even though they were hundreds of feet beneath the surface and sweating at their work. Small red hammers and sickles were the only insignia they wore. Unlike most sailors, the name of the submarine wasn't shown on their hats. They spoke Russian but the controls of the undersea vessel were all labeled in German.

The captain let the lad stay in the control room, in a corner out of the way, because he was eight years old, bright and curious. And because the captain had a son about the same age. The bulkheads smelled of fresh paint. The work space smelled of diesel oil and human sweat. Not a place preferred by Sam and Nell Margate, the other two passengers. Besides, they were not welcome there. They had been given the first officer's stateroom and were told to stay put, to keep out of the way.

"We'll be there soon, Geremy," Captain Evlanov called to the boy from the periscope where he stood most of the time. He spoke in Russian, their native tongue. "I can see the coast clearly. Maybe a half hour and you will be going ashore."

Geremy Margate, the name they had given him, re-

*mained silent, scared, knowing that what they were
doing was important. But he was scared as only a boy
can be of adult plans. It was one thing to play games, to
pretend. It was another to have parents picked out for
you, to be taught to speak English as if it were your
native tongue, and to be shipped thousands of miles
from home to live among strangers.*

*They had come in as close to shore as they could, just
around the south tip of Greenstone Point, away from
the British ships anchored on the other side of the point.*

*The submarine rose slowly to break the surface in the
coal-black darkness off the Scottish shore, wary of
patrols that swept the coast regularly. Sailors struggled
with an old fishing dinghy that had been lashed to the
conning tower. Sam Margate would row it ashore. The
boy had seen him practice back in Leningrad. It hadn't
been easy. Sam had lost a leg while serving on a Russian
minesweeper.*

*The captain nodded knowingly, saying his farewells
silently, as Geremy watched Sam climb up the conning
tower awkwardly. Nell followed, her skirts billowing in
the backdraft. She was going to be his mother and Sam
his father. He barely knew them, though he knew the
family history created for them as well as he'd known
his real family's.*

*The row to shore was a nightmare. They watched the
captured German submarine slip beneath the waves,
leaving them a half mile from shore. The chop was
almost four feet, a swell coming from shore, almost too
much for a one-legged man to overcome. It wasn't at all
like Leningrad.*

*Sam pushed his artificial leg against a rib of the boat
and heaved at the oars until they made headway. The
shore, a strip of barren, dark coast, started to loom
ahead of them, then started to recede.*

An offshore current held the dinghy from the shore. Sam pulled until his hands were raw, yet they made little progress. The bow yawed violently. They hadn't counted on the high chop or the offshore drift during practice runs back home.

Waves washed over the gunwales, leaving the bottom of the boat full of icy water. The boy had never been so frightened in his life.

Nell sat impatiently in the prow for fifteen minutes, giving Sam a chance to make it, then, almost sending the boat awash, she scrambled to the seat beside him, took one of the oars, and with arms and back more than a match for a man's, pulled her weight.

Her effort seemed to give Sam added strength. Slowly, the towering cliffs came closer, looming over them like an enormous black cape, darkening the rocks at the base of the cliffs.

Geremy bailed frantically with blood-streaked hands. After another half hour of torturous work, they reached shore.

Gnarled hands reached for the prow of the old dinghy as Nell and Sam, almost exhausted, pulled her to a deserted dock, the wood rotting, covered with caked salt. A few words were exchanged, in English, Sam using the cockney twang he'd studied so hard, the stranger speaking funny, rolling his r's, using words Geremy hadn't heard before.

The stranger tied up the boat and led them to the top along a treacherous path on the side of the rocky shore. It seemed an endless journey to Geremy, and worse for Sam with his wooden leg slipping on the salt-sprayed rock. But once at the top, the view was one the boy would never forget for the rest of his life.

Dawn was breaking at their backs as they looked down from the high cliff at the might of the Royal Navy

*spread out before them. This was Gruinard Bay, the
main refueling base for the northern fleet. Their cottage
was on the crest of the hill. For the rest of the war
Geremy would see the comings and goings of the fleet
and attend a one-room school in the town of Gruinard
along with the few children of local farmers. . . .*

The Right Honorable Geremy Farnsworth Margate
opened his eyes in the luxurious canopied bed. He
wasn't on the coast he'd seen for the first time so many
years ago. He was in the manor house at Dorking, south
of London, that he used when he could get away from
Parliament and his far-flung business interests. It was
an old manor house of seven bedrooms and four baths,
surrounded by a high wall, private and blanketed with
security.

He realized he'd had the dream again. But it wasn't a
dream. It was a remarkably clear memory of the most
traumatic period of his life. To be uprooted from
Mother Russia, given parents who were strangers, made
to live in a foreign land and grow up to be the same as
the foreign children—that had been the hardest part.

Sam, his "father," had watched the fleet and
reported his intelligence through a control at the local
pub. Ironically, Sam was treated like a hero by the
locals, the brave, one-legged veteran of the British fleet.
His cover was excellent and well rehearsed. He knew
more about the British navy than most swabbies.

Nell was sweet and friendly, and had soon been accepted by the matrons of a normally dour community.

After the war they had been given funds to move to
London. Money was always there when needed. In the
late forties Sam bought a clothing business and, with the
help of his control, expanded it to a large chain. He and
Nell had been chosen for their cunning. Things went

well for them. The plan was for them to become upper middle class and to educate their son with the sons of lords.

The hardest part for Geremy came after Oxford, when he was in his early twenties and starting to take over the business. Control had arranged for Sam and Nell to die in an auto crash and for their bodies to be burned beyond recognition. Of course, theirs were not the bodies in the crash. They were shipped home secretly, to be reassigned. Their eighteen years in the United Kingdom were finished. Geremy was on his own.

Now, more than a quarter of a century later, he lay in bed, his hands behind his head, and thought of his background again. The constant aloneness was perhaps the second most traumatic part. He had the businesses Sam had built. He had his friends from school to rally behind him, ones from the old boy network that would serve him the rest of his life. He had been captain of the debating team at Oxford. They had all said he would go into politics, not knowing it had been ordained for him in the Kremlin years ago.

Margate brought his mind back from Oxford and his graduation in the mid-fifties. Now it was the eighties, and he was fifty-one. He had built the clothing business into a conglomerate. He was a member of Parliament, a respected contributor to the present government, touted to be the next home secretary. It was time to worry about the present and not dwell on the past. The past could do him no good and could only do him harm. He had a job to do and it was going well. He was convinced, as his teachers had told him so long ago, that he had been born for the job.

He was tall, slightly overweight, had a leonine mass of hair turning gray, and had developed the complexion of an English country gentleman. He had blue eyes, crinkled at the corners. He looked the part of the country squire, the powerful businessman, and the M.P. equally well. And he had a destiny. One that went far beyond the roles he played so well. One that had been planned for him thousands of miles away.

He was brought out of his reverie by Beverley. She had swept into their bedroom like the commanding presence she was. She walked to the bed and smiled down at him.

"Have a nice sleep?" she asked.

"Just closed my eyes," he said.

"I wanted to talk to you about the new Gainsborough. Sotheby's will be shipping it tomorrow and we haven't decided where to hang it."

He looked around their bedroom, at the Matisse on the far wall, and the Gauguin to his left. The room was large, the furniture all antique, the contents of this room alone worth more than a million pounds.

"Must we buy more paintings?" he asked. "Seems to me it would be better to have a real need for something and then go buy it."

"The product of your plebian upbringing," she chided. "Are we short of money?"

"No," he said.

"Well, then. You leave the running of the house to me." She smiled as she moved toward the door. "Give it some thought, darling." She swept out the door just as the French-style phone rang at his ear.

He reached to the night table on his right and fumbled with the awkward receiver. "Yes?" he said.

"Squire?"

"Who's this?"

"Johnson at Achiltibuie."

"What the hell . . . ?" He had to restrain himself from shouting. "I told you not to call me here unless it was an emergency."

"It is an emergency."

"Wait a minute." Margate swung his feet off the bed and threw a small privacy switch on the base of the gilt and white phone. "Now, what is it?" he snapped.

"One of our people is missing. I've had a very discreet search party out looking. No luck."

"One of our imports or a local?" Margate asked.

"One of our own. A party man. Veteran of Afghanistan."

"So? Does that make him loyal?"

"I know this one. He'd never go wrong. I think he was taken," Johnson said.

Geremy Farnsworth Margate sat for a few seconds digesting the news. This project—he'd dubbed it Project Cavern—was the biggest thing he'd ever planned for the party. He was extremely vulnerable, but it was worth the risk and he'd covered his tracks as much as he could. "Tell me about it," he said.

"The last one we had to dispose of wasn't a local. Now we've got one come up in a car and taken a room in the village. Been asking questions at the pub."

"I don't like it. What does Penny think?" he asked.

"Sergeant Penny doesn't think. He's an ass. I think we made a mistake with him," Johnson said.

"*You* made a mistake. *You*, Johnson. *You* disposed of the boy and the old man. Now you've messed with a stranger and someone's come to find out why his friend disappeared. This one's sure to be official. We've got to find a way to stop him. Any ideas?"

Johnson didn't respond for a few seconds.

"I'm coming up. Send a helicopter to Prestwick for me."

• • •

Hawk dialed an overseas number using a phone he kept locked in a bottom drawer of his desk. Beside the phone he kept a small directory. It contained the very private numbers of his counterparts around the world. Some, he seldom called. Some, like Franklin Hargreaves, head of MI5, he called often.

The phone rang at the other end ten times. Hawk was about to hang up when a female voice answered. It had to be Hargreave's secretary. No one else knew about the phone.

"David Hawk. Franklin was spotted at Dulles as he came in. Where is he now?" he asked without preliminaries.

"Are you in Washington?" she asked.

"Yes."

"He's at the British embassy." She gave him an unlisted number there.

Hawk dialed the second number, gave his name, and waited.

"Hargreaves," a cultured voice finally said. It was a voice Hawk immediately recognized.

"You're on my home turf without calling? Were we going to have lunch?" Hawk chided.

"Sorry, old chap. Was going to call you tomorrow. What's up?"

"Can we talk on this line?"

"This end is clean," Hargreaves said.

"Your P.M. has given this one to our president. She's bypassed you and it's my ass if it gets out."

"I'll be damned! She's never done this before as far as I know."

"I think she's afraid of another scandal within her party. That's what it looks like," Hawk said. "If she gave it to you, Fleet Street would get on to it."

"Could be. Too many leaks. What's it all about?"

Hawk told him what Carter had discovered and what they suspected. "We need to know who bought up the land," he said. "I suspect this man, the one in your government, bought it through a front."

"A mole? You think he's a mole?" Hargreaves asked.

"Too soon to tell. But it sure as hell looks like it," Hawk sighed.

"I'll get my best people on it right away."

"One more thing," Hawk said. "I've got to ask you to keep strictly clear. If the P.M. found out you're involved, she'd have both our asses."

"Don't concern yourself, old man. Mum's the word."

"And I'll probably need you for a cleanup job at the end," Hawk added.

"No problem. You'll be at your office?" Hargreaves asked.

"As far as I know. If I have to get involved personally, I'll be at the Dorchester in London."

"I'll call you before I leave. No chance for a meet this time around," Hargreaves said.

Hawk wasn't about to ask what he was doing in Washington. If Hargreaves had wanted Hawk to know, he would have told him.

He hung up and sat thinking about Carter. Where did all these masterminds come from? Had this one been in the woodwork all along, waiting to emerge and do damage?

He'd seen them come and go for more than forty years. A man should tire of it. But he didn't. It got to him when he lost a good man like Hood. But he couldn't imagine doing anything else.

•   •   •

It was starting to turn dark as the chopper set down on the lawn in front of the huge manor house at Achiltibuie. The old house was covered with hardy vines that resisted all the wind's efforts to dislodge them, and dark green leaves had taken over the exterior. The interior was like a Scandinavian hunting lodge, all beams and stucco, boars' heads and antlers. It had been built by a Norwegian merchant king years ago and picked up cheaply by Margate when he'd decided to go ahead with Project Cavern.

The house was unique for many reasons. One was the wine cellars the Norwegian had blasted out of the rock before starting to build. They were deep and forbidding. For wine, they'd turned out to be too cold and damp. For dungeons, they were ideal.

"Where is the stranger now?" Margate asked Johnson when they were settled in a room he used as an office. He spoke in Russian. He could only use his native tongue infrequently, when at the northern house, and when he was with someone like Johnson. He felt the need of it, a tie with home.

"At the local pub again, pumping the locals," Johnson said. He was a huge man, muscular except for a rounded belly. He stood well over six feet six and weighed almost three hundred pounds.

"But they know nothing," Margate said.

"As far as we know," Johnson said, his green eyes turning from Margate's.

"You think he took our man?" Margate asked, taking a long cigar from a humidor and lighting it without offering one to his aide.

"I think he did," Johnson said, running a massive hand through unruly red hair. "He brushed out his tire tracks, but we found evidence of a struggle in an old barn."

Margate puffed on the cigar and thought about the cost of failure. "He interrogated and killed him?" he asked.

"We think so."

"He's a professional?"

"We're sure he has to be. No amateur would be able to go down the cliff and pick off one of our men like a fish."

"Then what did he do—after taking our man?" Margate asked, the germ of a plan forming in his mind.

"He went to the room he'd rented. The woman was up. My people stayed close," he said, taking out a pack of cigarettes and lighting one. "They reported the two of them talked and drank."

"He's an American, you said?"

"That's what our contact at the pub told me."

"Good. Like the British, he'll be a sentimentalist. We'll take the woman and make him come to us," Margate said and grinned.

"Two problems with that. He might not come. He might call in his people. It's coming out in the open too much."

"I don't agree. You were the ones to call attention to us. Now we've got to get our hands on this one—alive. And soon. Get him to talk. Find out what's going on in the enemy camp."

"If you say so. But it could backfire. I'm—"

"*Just do it!*" Margate ordered. "Pick up the woman!"

"Where do you want her?" Johnson asked, subdued.

"Here! What the hell's the matter with you? Do you want to give her a guided tour of our project?"

FOUR

Smoke drifted up to the rafters from the old men's pipes and Carter's cigarette as they drank and talked. The tables had been pulled into a circle. Carter had become popular at the pub. He swapped stories with the old boys, trying to outdo them, not letting them put their hands in their pockets to fill their glasses. Eventually, they ceased to try.

He raised his fourth pint for the night, burped, and pushed the chipped mug away. "No more for me. Got to get on the road."

"Staying with Mrs. Wyness, be you?" one asked.

"Yes. Good bed and better food," he said, rising to leave. "See you tomorrow."

"Best bed in town, I'd bet," the oldest of the men said, cackling with glee.

"I wouldn't know," Carter answered with a laugh as he headed for the door.

It was about three hundred yards from the pub to the cottage. The moon was full and shone on the river, turning the water from black to silver in places as it rushed through town on its way to the sea. The few houses he passed were quiet, some with dim lights in the windows, a few with TV antennas on the roof to pull in weak signals from Inverness.

The little house was dark. The rented Rover sat in the

driveway in shadow. Perhaps Mary had gone to bed early. Carter used his key and walked into the house quietly, lighting a small lamp in the living room.

They had been there and hadn't tried to cover their tracks. Some furniture had been knocked over, and the books and magazines that had been on the coffee table lay scattered on the floor. The struggle had been short.

Carter cursed under his breath. They were professionals. They were smart. They figured the sentimental American would come after the woman.

They were right. They were so damned right. But they didn't know Nick Carter. He would go after her all right, but not the way they expected.

Carter jogged back to the pub and entered, trying not to look concerned. He sat with the men and put his head low, toward the middle of the table, speaking in confidence. They all leaned forward, sensing what he had to say was important.

"You've all guessed what I am," he said conspiratorially.

They all nodded.

"I don't want you involved, but I need your help in one thing."

"What is it, mate?" Jock Fraser asked. He had liked Geoff Hood and sat with the group whenever Carter was there.

"I need a boat. Something I can use in the bay. Something strong and quiet. Maybe a small diesel fishing boat."

They looked from one to the other, then at Fraser.

"Got what you need," the younger man said. "I'll take you to it."

"One other thing," Carter said, rising to leave.

"We've had three deaths that we know of. Someone is out there—someone deadly. I don't want to scare you, but be careful. Stay away from the cliffs at night. Stay away from the new fence."

He turned to leave, then turned back. Fraser waited for him at the door. "Two more things," he said, his tone leaving no doubt about the gravity of the situation. "I don't want any of you being heroes. And I want you to be very wary of strangers. Sergeant Penny is handling this for you. That's his choice. But he could also be one of them—any one of you could be. So watch your backs. Let me know if you learn anything."

As they left the pub and were immediately enfolded in the dark as clouds covered the moon, Fraser asked the inevitable: "You really think we've got something evil here?"

"Yes. But you've all got to keep your nerve. And stay out of it," he warned. "Remind the others to keep their cool and stay out of it."

"And one of us could be a spy?"

"Any one of you, yes. That's the way they work. Infiltrate. Divide and conquer," Carter said. "Ask yourself why Sergeant Penny hasn't called in help. He's either very stupid and proud, or he's one of them."

He hadn't wanted to reveal himself to the locals. He hadn't wanted to get a lot of innocent civilians hurt, or killed. But he was just too obvious in their midst. There was no way he could hide what he was. He had to play it this way; he didn't have much choice.

They had been walking on a track leading to the river. At a house two hundred yards from the pub and about as far from the Wyness house, Fraser walked around back to a boathouse that was almost falling down around itself. He pulled open a creaking door and turned on a weak, naked bulb.

A wooden-hulled boat bobbed in the shallow river water. She was painted black. The paint had chipped in spots to show the original light blue. She had a small superstructure amidships and a diesel housing aft.

Fraser grinned sheepishly in the dull light. "Painted her black for poaching," he said. "Damned landowners have all the fishing rights. Ain't right."

Carter estimated she was twenty feet at the waterline. The gunwales were three feet from the dark water lapping at her sides.

"Diesel okay?" he asked.

"Best thing about her. Smooth and quiet. Not built for speed, but they won't hear you coming," the Scotsman said, grinning.

Carter handed over five hundred pounds. "I'll give you five hundred more when I'm finished. If she's damaged, I'll pay for a new boat."

"Forget it. This lot's enough—too much," he said. "I don't want to know what you're doing," he said as he handed Carter a key. "I just hope you get the bloody bastards."

The black fatigues were still in the back of the car, bird droppings and all. Carter carried them into the house, donned a wet suit under them, and transferred his weapons. He moved from the darkened house to the boathouse, opened the doors leading to the black water boiling down from the mountains, and inserted the key.

The diesel churned to life. He revved her for a few seconds and let her settle down to a contented idle. She purred like a kitten.

With all the skill he'd garnered over the years, he reversed the old boat, eased her out of the boathouse into the stream, and found himself being forced toward the sea, despite being in reverse.

He didn't have to worry about being under way and having control. He gave the diesel minimum forward revs and stayed in the middle of the channel, letting the river take him out to sea as smartly as a cork in rivulets of rain.

The moon stayed behind clouds that were gathering for a storm. As he entered salt water, he felt more than the spray from the waves breaking against the cliffs. A fine mist was coming down, cutting down his visibility and adding camouflage to his presence. He thanked whatever gods were looking down on him.

The Ewe River flowed from Loch Marie to Loch Ewe and out to sea. Loch Ewe was more like a narrow bay. It was salt water, south of Gruinard Bay, and not visible to the enemy.

Carter opened up the revs as the boat took him out to open water. He rounded Greenstone Point and was into Gruinard Bay before the owner had called "Time, boys" at the pub.

He stayed close to the southwest cliffs of the bay. As he remembered, the opening he'd seen was about halfway between the villages of Aultbea and Gruinard. He held the tiller with his knees, making about three knots, and raised his binoculars to take a look.

He was about five miles away and on course.

The closer the fishing boat eased toward the sub pens, the darker the scene became. Carter was sailing her without riding lights. He'd been on the water a half hour, and his night vision was sharp.

The man on guard duty looked out to sea and up at

the cliffside occasionally. He never turned his glasses to the waters close at hand.

Carter kept as close to the jutting rocks as possible, moving at less than two knots. Finally he found a shelf of rock in a recess about a hundred yards from the sentry and out of line of his sight. In the darkness beneath the towering cliffs, he secured the boat to scrub pine growing between the rocks and crept toward the opening.

The rock was slippery underfoot as he crept close to the sub pens. He followed the same path he'd used before. The sentry didn't see him coming.

It wasn't easy. It never was. The sentry was huge, a giant. His features looked Slavic under the wool cap. Ridges of bone hooded his eye sockets. He had prominent cheekbones, protruding ears, and a granite slab of bone for a chin.

Carter was patient. He waited until the guard turned from him, then slipped behind him to deliver a karate chop to one side of his neck.

The giant dropped like a stone.

Carter caught the man's assault rifle before it hit the ground. It was of Finnish design, better than the Russian-made ones, a deadly weapon.

The man would be out for a half hour. Carter had time to look around if no one else checked on the guard. The sub pens went back as far as he could see. One of the subs was less than a hundred feet from the entrance. It wasn't as small as he'd thought, about a hundred feet long—miniature when compared to conventional nuclear subs, but big enough and a dangerous weapons carrier. Its conning tower was sheet steel, but immediately below it the superstructure was transparent, a kind of observation room. Obviously the underwater craft hadn't been intended for deep-sea work. But the captured guard had told him they had stealth capability, able to move undetected within the range of electronic detection devices. Depth wasn't a factor.

He could see another conning tower behind the first and another beyond that. The cavern was huge and poorly lighted. No one appeared to be about.

Without warning, two guards emerged from the first sub, followed by a man in a lab coat. They saw Carter and opened fire. Their Finnish-made automatic sub-machine guns chewed chunks from the rock over his head as he ducked. The sound of their rapid fire reverberated around the rock walls of the cavern.

Carter's Luger slipped easily from its holster. The gun was an extension of his hand as she began to buck. Holes appeared in the foreheads of the two guards who went down as blood and bone chips covered the lab coat of the third man.

Carter leaped for the railing of the deck. He knew he had little time. Someone had to have heard the racket. He had to get to the third man and get away.

The man was obviously petrified by the firefight. At first he cowered near the conning tower, then he jumped for the hatch.

Carter knew he had to take him prisoner. The man was probably a technician and knew a lot more about the installation than any guard. The Killmaster sprang for the hatch as the man disappeared down the opening.

It was close. The wheel was spinning the round hatch closed when Carter got there. A tug-of-war followed: Carter tried to turn the wheel to the left; the man below desperately tried to turn it to the right.

Carter slowly overpowered the man. As the wheel turned in his hand he could hear noises at the back of the cavern, men's voices and running feet.

The wheel reached the end of the threading and the hatch came open in his powerful hands. The man in the lab coat was still hanging on. Carter grabbed him by the arm with one hand and pulled him through.

The noises were louder now. Carter clipped the man behind the ear and threw him over one shoulder in a fireman's carry.

Whoever was coming started to fire wildly before they got to the opening. Slugs ricocheted off stone walls and cut through the water. Showers of chipped rock followed Carter as he ran.

He was almost through the opening, his prisoner on his back, their silhouettes clear against the light.

As he glanced back he saw them—men in olive uniforms with the same bright crest he'd seen before. The guards hesitated, afraid to fire on the scientist. In that split second of hesitation, Carter was through, out into the night and the fury of crashing waves against rock.

The rock was a cruel master to conquer. He fell twice, dropping his bundle on the way back. The boat was tied by knots that slipped loose at a tug. The old diesel caught and turned them away from the cavern.

The boat's top speed was ten knots. With his prisoner lying in the bottom of the boat, the man from AXE kept close under the shelf of rock—as close to the wave-crashed slimy wall as he could. The prisoner's condition worried Carter. Blood was running from the cuts and scrapes he'd received when Carter had dropped him.

But he couldn't worry about the man now. Glancing back, he saw a power boat, its spotlights already searching the water, coming on strong. It took off straight out to sea without seeing the old black boat keeping close to the rock.

As he turned her around Greenstone Point, Carter glanced again and saw the pursuit out at sea, her spotlights swinging in ever-increasing arcs. Within minutes, the scarred rock that was the point closed off the scene and he was into Loch Ewe.

The scene was peaceful as Carter cruised up the Ewe River at midnight. He brought the boat around smartly, against the current and into her old wooden home, as if he'd done it a thousand times.

Before he took his prisoner to the house, Carter made a sweep of the area. He saw nothing. But he decided the house was not the place. He went back for the still unconscious man, hefted him onto his shoulder once more, and took off at a lope across untended fields, keeping away from the road.

FIVE

Carter had to call on all his prodigious strength to make it to the cliffside far away from the populated area. He had to skirt the pub and round one of the enormous rocky hills to make it to the cliffs looking down on Loch Ewe. His white-coated burden hadn't stirred, but the technician's weight seemed to multiply as the trek stretched to almost four miles.

The back of the rock hill was dotted with hundreds of crevasses, some small, others quite large. Carter was starting to breathe hard. He didn't need to go further. The ridges that provided footholds were starting to disappear, and he was far enough from anyone to assure privacy.

The crevass he chose was twenty feet across and thirty feet deep. An uneven floor had formed over the years as rubble tumbled from the roof and sides. Animal droppings were fresh and ripe, adding a strong aroma to the musty smell. The opening looked out on the widest part of Loch Ewe, almost at its juncture with the sea. The scene, far from the tavern and the enemy, was floodlit by a moon free of passing clouds.

Carter dropped the man on a flat spot just inside the opening and sat to rest, smoking a cigarette, looking out on the landscape. He was not looking forward to what he had to do. The man had to know where the woman was. He would have to tell.

Ten minutes later, Carter flipped what was left of the cigarette down toward the sea and reached for the leather case of drugs. His prisoner was beginning to stir. The curtain was about to go up.

The leather case wasn't there. Carter searched all the pockets of his black coveralls without finding it. The case containing the syringes must have slipped out during one of his encounters with the guards or on the way up the clliff. He swore out loud.

Carter slapped the man awake and watched as he slowly sat up and looked around. He was of medium height and weight, with a thin face and soft hands. His skin was unusually white, matching the sparse hair that blew in the wind that whistled in from the sea. He looked with fear at his captor.

Carter flipped his stiletto from its chamois hiding place to his right palm in one fluid motion. The moon caught the metal in a flash of light and drew the Russian's eyes.

"This can be easy or as hard as you want to make it," Carter said in English.

The man shook his head and moved away a couple of feet, his eyes wild, staring, almost popping from their sockets.

Carter repeated his warning in Russian.

"What is it you want?" the man asked, his voice weak, his speech garbled, as if his tongue were unwilling to obey his will.

"Perhaps many things. It depends on who you are and what you know," Carter said coldly, moving the stiletto back and forth, flashing reflected light at his prisoner. "First, I want to know what they did with the woman," Carter said, his voice as much a threat as the knife.

The man moved further away, his back coming up against the rock. "I don't know of any woman," he said, his eyes fixed on the gleam of metal in Carter's hand.

Too fast for the man to react, Carter moved to him, circled his neck with one arm, and shoved the point of the stiletto behind his left ear. He let the captive scream. The cry of fear floated out into the sea breeze. It carried out and down to Loch Ewe like a banshee's wail.

"You know about the man who runs your project. Tell me about him."

The man tried to press himself against the wall, away from the knife, without answering.

"When he's here, does he stay in the cavern?" Carter demanded, his mouth next to the man's ear.

The prisoner still didn't answer. Carter pressed the knife harder. The scream that followed was enough to send a shiver down a strong man's spine.

"No! Don't push it further!" the man whimpered. "No . . . he . . . he has a house," he said, his chest rising and falling, his breathing strained, his heartbeat rapid.

"Where is it? Have you been there? Would he take a prisoner there to question her?" Carter asked in quick succession.

"Yes. We have meetings there sometimes."

"Where!"

"On the cliff . . . just north of Achiltibuie . . . alone on the cliff . . . big house like a lodge . . . Scandinavian owned it . . . they took the boy there to question him."

"Who is your leader? His name? What does he look like?" Carter shouted over a strong wind that had blown up.

"I've never seen him," the man said weakly.

"You're lying!" Carter shouted, and moved the point

of his knife as if preparing to thrust it directly into the man's ear.

A scream of terror fought with the wind for release and drifted out to sea. The smell of urine joined the other odors in the crevass.

"Tell me. Or the knife goes in all the way. You said you had meetings there. Now, what is his name?"

"They call . . . we call him the Squire. I don't . . . I don't know his name."

"Who is he?"

"Don't know . . . but he's rich . . . powerful . . . heard someone say he was political." The words came out faintly as if the man was finished already.

"Politics in Russia or here?"

"Here."

"What does he look like?" the Killmaster demanded. He hated this kind of session, but it had to be done. The man was a scientist working covertly in a foreign land. He had to take his risks like everyone else.

"He's . . . tall . . . overweight, has a lot of hair . . . turning gray . . . blue eyes . . . wrinkles around his eyes . . . deep wrinkles."

"Tell me about your work," Carter asked. He had done well. Anything else would be a bonus.

"I can't . . . one thing they tell us . . . nothing about the work."

Carter pressed the needlelike point of the knife against the inside of the man's ear.

Again, a mournful wail floated out into the night. Anyone walking the cliffs would have been frightened silly by the sound.

"If I push further, you're a dead man," the Killmaster whispered in the man's other ear. "It's not too far to the brain."

"I helped design the craft . . . hundred feet long . . . nuclear-powered . . . plexiglass below the conning tower . . . cruises only to four hundred feet, but has diving bell . . . nuclear missiles."

"Is it able to escape detection?" Carter asked.

"How . . . ? Who told you that?" the scientist gasped.

"Never mind. Just answer the questions. Is this the only base?" Carter demanded.

"Please don't ask any more. I can't tell you. They'll kill . . . kill me." The voice was weak, as if the man were about to pass out.

Carter knew he could get very little more. "Have you worked on any other bases?" he persisted, turning the knife slightly.

The body shuddered in his grasp. "Near Singapore . . . up the coast toward Bangkok . . . about a hundred miles. Hong Kong island . . . west side of Aberdeen town," the man said with the last of his strength.

Carter relaxed his arm as it started to cramp. He'd had little rest and his muscles were sore from the climbing.

As he relaxed, the Russian made a sudden move to get away. He jerked his head to the side quickly—and into the knife. Blood rushed from his ear down the hilt of the stiletto as the body convulsed and was still.

Carter cursed to himself. He was alone. The man was dead.

The descent was easy by comparison. He had cleaned Hugo and tossed the Russian's body into the sea. His destination was the pub.

He reached the back door out of breath, his black fatigues smeared with the dead man's blood.

The owner, Jack Brodie, had been in bed. He

answered the door with a shotgun in his hand. He almost used it before recognizing Carter.

"I have to use your telephone. It's urgent," Carter said.

Brodie opened the door, shouted upstairs for his wife to go back to bed, and let Carter into a small kitchen. He had a telephone on a table where he kept his accounting records.

"What the hell happened to you, man?" he asked.

"Can't tell you now, but I will when it's all over. Now, let me use the phone alone, okay?"

"All right. But you look like you've been butchering some lambs," he said, then blanched as he realized the blood would be human.

Carter sat at the phone as the inn's owner turned on his heel and headed upstairs. He punched in his recognition codes that would put him into the AXE worldwide communications network. A synthesized voice answered.

"Amalgamated. Hello, Nick. Can I be of service?"

The honeyed tones of the sexy female voice was one of Hawk's little jokes. The network was one of his better ideas, but the sultry electronic receptionist never failed to annoy Carter.

"I need Hawk right away. Urgent."

He had to admit that the automated communications system worked well. When he told the machine his business was urgent, he got results. He waited no more than a few seconds to hear Hawk's voice. It would be about ten at night in Washington.

"N3. What's up?" The voice of the crusty older man demanded.

"I've learned more about the man they call the Squire. He's a powerful businessman—fifties, a full head of gray hair, tall, overweight, ruddy complexion, blue eyes, prominent crow's feet. He may be in British politics. He owns a large house or lodge, Scandinavian design, north of a town called Achiltibuie on the north-east cliffs of Gruinard Bay. Sounds like the Soviets turned him early or he's a mole.''

"What are your plans now?" Hawk asked.

"Get inside the pens, plant explosives, destroy the place," he lied. He wasn't ready to tell his boss he was going after Mary Wyness. Hawk didn't approve of him risking his life and a project to save civilians.

"I'm already checking on the top man. I'll feed this information to my contact. I should have everything on him in about twelve hours."

"Okay. I'll hold off. I'll call you," Carter said, hanging up. Hawk's plan would give him time to get into the lodge and look for Mary.

He turned to find Brodie coming down the stairs again. The man hadn't been listening; he was concerned about Carter's welfare.

"Can I get you anything, lad? A hot cup of tea?" he asked.

"No, thanks. I've got a lot of work to do before dawn. Maybe I'll see you for breakfast."

He headed for the door, leaving the owner looking after him, shaking his head.

Back at the house, cloud cover was starting to thin, but the car was in shadow. Sweating and splattered with blood, Carter eased himself under one fender at the front of the car and swung his penlight around the frame looking for a booby trap. This was the one place they knew to look for him. It would be easy enough to stop him before he got too close.

He found nothing. Perhaps an exploding car was too obvious. It was bad enough that three people were missing; a bomb blast could not be overlooked. Sergeant Penny would have to call in Scotland Yard for something like that.

He opened the trunk and pulled a clean set of black fatigues from his bag. He changed in the pale light of the moon, slipped on his weapons, and blackened his face.

He closed up the car again and started out with his long, distance-devouring lope toward the old boat-house.

The slow ride downriver was repeated. The moon stayed behind clouds. No one could see the black boat or the man unless he knew exactly where to look.

Carter stood at the back of the small cabin's superstructure, looking straight ahead, one hand on the tiller. He rounded Greenstone Point and saw only the open sea and whitecaps on the three-foot chop. No boats were in sight. No spotlights cut through the black of night.

The opposite shore was a good five or six miles across, according to an old map he'd found on the boat. He revved her to her full ten knots and headed straight for the opposite shore.

The room she was in had to be very large. She could hear the sounds, the soft echoes of small scurrying animals reverberating off the walls. Mary shuddered at the thought, but she could do nothing. Once or twice an animal had run across her feet and she had screamed. With her hands and legs bound by stout rope, screaming was about all she could do. Screaming gave her an outlet for her fury and her fear.

She was alone, her skin damp, her throat raw. The room was so dark her night vision showed her almost nothing. Perhaps there was nothing to see—a room undistinguished by the presence of anything but stone walls and floors, the moisture of seepage, the smell of mildew and rot.

They had left her alone. She had expected to be manhandled, possibly raped, but they obviously wanted her for something else. Perhaps as bait.

Nick Carter.

They knew he would come.

She thought about her boarder. She knew he was something special, something other than he pretended to be. Something about him . . . mysterious . . . worldly. He would come, and they would get him.

For the first time since they took her, she started to cry.

The shore came at him like a monstrous humpbacked prehistoric being sleeping in the distance. Lights appeared off to starboard on his right. He headed for them.

It was a village. Probably ten or fifteen houses, but only one had a light showing in the middle of the night. Someone sick. Or someone who read when sleep wouldn't come.

He turned the tiller to port, cruising slowly up the coast. He steered a mile toward the sea, then another.

Suddenly he saw it. A huge lodge, all stucco and hewn planks, standing on the edge of an insurmountable rock face. Most of the structure was overgrown with ivy. He took the boat back to the village dock, tied up, and ran back to the house.

The lodge was surrounded by a stone fence from cliffside on the south to cliffside on the north. Carter climbed a twisted, wind-blown tree and scanned the grounds with his glasses.

Two men patrolled the front. He could see shadows at

the back, but he couldn't see the men. There were probably two at the back. He couldn't know how many were inside.

The man he wanted to destroy was inside, either expecting him, or confident he was safe against one man. The Squire was about to find out he wasn't impregnable. The Englishman would keep for another night, but his prisoner was about to exit.

Carter considered scaling the rock face, but decided against it. It would be an exhausting climb and he would still have to get by the guards outside.

He vaulted noiselessly from the tree to the top of the wall. When the guards were all patrolling with their back to him, he leaped down to the lawn and crept toward the house.

It was all going too well. He had a strange feeling between his shoulder blades.

Suddenly, a flame in cupped hands appeared ten feet in front of him. A lone man lit a cigarette, standing in an open door. Carter was on him, knocked him senseless, and was in the house without making a sound.

The center room was as large as some of the casinos in Las Vegas, so large the perspective of the walls was like two lines coming together in the distance. Stags' heads covered the rough board ceiling—hundreds of them. Boars' heads and bear pelts decorated the rest of the cavernous room.

A balcony ran along all four sides. Circular wooden staircases were dotted along the balcony—at least four of them. Huge clusters of lights hung from between the animal heads, and in miniature from beneath the balconies. Bedrooms or small rooms for storage and linens could be seen beyond the balcony. An immense fireplace on one wall was crafted of native stone. It had to be twenty feet across, ten feet high, with a firebox at least ten by five. Even with these dimensions, it was small for the size of the room.

Carter saw no one in either the main room or on the balcony.

Where to start? Did the old place have a wine cellar? Would they put her down there or in one of the scores of small rooms upstairs? He decided his best chance was downstairs.

Carter skirted the huge room, conscious of the uneasy feeling that wouldn't go away. He found no stairway to the lower level until he examined the fireplace. To one side, next to the pile of firewood, a small door led downstairs.

Carter opened the door slowly, started to pull it toward him, when a sharp pain attacked one hip.

He half turned. A tall man with a leonine mane of graying hair held a tranquilizer gun in his hand. He was smiling, which emphasized the crow's feet at the corners of his blue eyes.

Carter started to pull the dart from his hip and felt himself start to fall. The stairs punished him as he started down, but a darkness closed over him and he was in free fall, down a spinning vortex into oblivion.

SIX

"I don't like this, Comrade Margate," a short man in a white lab coat said. He resembled some kind of rodent, complete with beady eyes and protruding upper teeth. Breath whistled through the long yellow front teeth, making his *s*'s sound like a small steam whistle. "Moscow will not like it. First the boy; then the policeman." He paused to make his point, shaking a tobacco-stained finger. "Now it's up to five and you can't seem to control it."

They were in an office at the back of the house. Margate had set it up like a board room, complete with a table capable of seating twelve. In one corner, a huge oak table, antique and highly polished, was his control center when he was up north. A second office, smaller, housed an assistant, a young woman who had many skills, both secretarial and physical. This night they were only four: Margate, Johnson, and two scientists, Yuri Gregarov and Valeri Berof.

"You're too nervous, Gregarov. You purists from the National Academy always are," Margate said, the crow's feet at his eyes crinkling more than ever. He sounded confident but looked tired and worried.

"And you people have been here too long. You forget your training," the scientist shot back.

Johnson and Berof remained silent, letting the two men settle their own differences. Margate was the local man, in total charge and responsible to Moscow.

"We have it under control. The two downstairs will be interrogated and eliminated," Margate said. "I have a man coming in from Moscow tomorrow. An expert. I'll talk to them myself tonight. In my own way," he added with a cruel twist to his mouth.

"I demand to know what you intend to do," Gregarov said, his voice rising. "You are jeopardizing the whole project."

Margate changed from the outwardly benevolent politician to a man of stone. "Now, you listen and listen well." He spoke in Russian, his words clear and penetrating. "I have been underground for more than forty years. Johnson for almost thirty. Damn you and your project! Dammit to hell if we have to!" He picked up an empty glass and slopped some water into it from a pitcher. In his fury, the water spilled down his jowls as he drank in a hurry. "Do you think we're fools? You sit in your ivory towers of learning and don't know what the hell goes on outside."

He combed his bush of hair with splayed fingers and tried to calm himself. "I'm in charge of this operation and don't you ever forget it. I'm the most important tool we have in the United Kingdom. If I closed down the project and sent your body home in a box, with apologies, it would be understood." He looked the small man in the eye and grinned evilly. "In the most important circles in Moscow, it would be understood and accepted. Is that clear, comrade?"

"I didn't mean to question your authority, Comrade Margate," Gregarov said, his voice almost a whisper. "I merely wanted to know what you intended to do."

"Then I will tell you," Margate said in his most courtly manner, sitting up straight and leaning across

the table. "We will obtain a goat—a red herring—
someone to take the blame—a minor criminal from the
slums of Glasgow or Edinburgh. Sergeant Penny will
find him on the cliffs and will shoot him as he tries to
escape."

"It is too simple. They will never buy it." Berof
spoke for the first time. He was a man of middle height
and weight, nondescript when he wanted to be, a scientist. Unknown to the others, he was also a colonel in the
KGB. "The last one we shot off the cliff and the two
downstairs were not locals. Someone will be curious,"
he said. He was the youngest of the four, handsome and
assured. Margate valued his judgment. Unlike Gregarov, he was seldom emotional, used good judgment,
and almost never complained.

"The local M.P. is in my pocket," Margate explained. "He is related to Sergeant Penny—a cousin.
When they have the body of the criminal on ice, they
will hold a press conference. Their story will be that the
dead man was on the run, scrounging for food and
shelter, and killed to survive."

"And the two downstairs?" Berof asked. "What if
they are connected—from an agency?"

"I intend to find out myself," Margate told them. "If
I fail, we'll be fairly sure they're professionals. Our in-
terrogator will find out."

"He's from Serbsky? From that hellhole where they
train them all?" Johnson asked.

"Where else?" Margate said. "They're the best."

A strong man and a loyal one, Johnson nevertheless
shuddered at the thought. "I can't stand those bastards.
They're not human," he said. "They don't give a damn
for human life. Fry a brain for the joy of it."

Berof looked at Johnson with suspicion, making a

mental note to have him put under surveillance. But it was Margate who spoke.

"Fear is a prime ingredient, my dear fellow," Margate said and laughed. "Fear precedes them and they have a psychological advantage." He finished the glass of water, this time with a slowness that added to his emphasis. "Add to that their fantastic skills with drugs, and well . . ." The big man left the sentence unfinished.

"I don't like the idea of you interrogating them alone, before the expert gets here," Gregarov said, his tone neutral. He had learned his lesson. He wasn't about to have another direct confrontation.

"Alone it's going to be," Margate said. "Don't worry about me. They are secured firmly. No chance of them getting loose. I'm not going to touch their bonds. Besides, we're all entitled to our fun. It's my turn and it's been a long time."

Carter opened his eyes, shook his head. For several seconds he had been hearing someone call his name: "Carter! Carter! Nick . . . are you all right?"

It was Mary. He had found her. But where the hell were they? It was pitch-black. He looked straight ahead and could see nothing. The place smelled damp. He could hear the scratching of small claws at irregular intervals.

Gradually he began to see things close to him. He was strapped naked into a wooden chair, his arms out in front of him secured with leather straps to a hinged shelf at the front of his chair. His legs were parted, secured at the ankles. The way he was positioned, his testicles were displayed on a flat surface. The whole rig looked like an ancient torture instrument.

"Mary?" he called. "Speak again. Where are you?"

he croaked, his throat dry.

"Right in front of you. About twenty feet." Her voice was weak as if she had almost given up hope. "I'm so glad you are here. Oh, I don't know what I mean . . . it's been hell alone."

"It's okay," he said, knowing it wasn't. "We'll get out of this somehow."

He looked up in the darkness and as his night vision improved, he could see her clearly. She was also naked and on another strange contraption, her legs spread revealingly. Her ankles and wrists were tied with rope. Dried blood covered the bonds where she had fought to get loose. Her face was bruised and swollen. Despite her beatings, she struggled to release herself. He could see her muscles straining to release her arms.

"Did you see me fall, or did they carry me in?" he asked. He wanted to know where they were in relation to the door and the stairs where he'd tumbled. The first rule was to get the lay of the land. And you never gave up hope. If he'd not followed these rules, he'd have been dead long ago.

"I heard you fall. The next room, I think. I saw them carry you in and take your things."

"Did they take my weapons upstairs?" he asked.

"They didn't stop to put them anywhere down here. Two men helped the man who attacked you and they all left up the stairs right away. I heard the door close."

"Good. Did they hurt you, Mary? I mean . . . did they . . . ?"

"No. Nothing like that. They slapped me around, but they realized I didn't know anything. They've left me alone for hours. It's an awful place, Nick. A basement of some kind . . . all rock . . . cold and wet. I don't understand. I don't know what they wanted next. It was as if they were waiting for you."

"They were. I knew you were the bait, but I wasn't careful enough."

He could hear her sob and saw the tears course down her face. "Don't cry, Mary. It's not over until it's over, right?"

"Yogi Berra's philosophy. Sure. He was probably right. But you look like a trussed hunk of meat and I'm displayed like something from a raunchy skin magazine," she said. "They could do anything they want."

"Exactly," a third voice offered.

They had been so engrossed in their conversation, they hadn't heard the man approach. He had a full head of gray hair and piercing blue eyes. In the darkness, they could see him carrying some rusted old pieces of metal in one hand.

He put the objects in front of Carter, on the shelf next to the Killmaster's bound hands, and moved off to throw a light switch.

Two bare bulbs cast dim light over the scene, but it was enough to hurt their eyes. Carter noticed that Mary was dirty, as if she'd been dragged to the chair. Her hair was a mess. Mascara had flowed from her eyes down her cheeks to her chin. The bruises were ugly, turning black.

His eyes wandered to the objects before him. No. He didn't believe it. This was out of the Dark Ages.

"You like my tools?" Margate asked. "Found them in an old chest left down here. The original owner must have been a real character. Often wonder who he used them on."

The objects were tangled together but were unmistakable. Carter had seen them in a chamber of horrors as a kid and at the Tower Bridge display in London.

"You've got to be kidding," he said. "Thumbscrews went out with the Middle Ages."

"And the steel cap. Don't forget the steel cap." The big man laughed. "And the nut crusher. I've been wanting to try that one out."

Carter looked at the rusted instruments and knew he was in for a hard time. He wasn't afraid of talking. He'd been worked over by experts before and in situations worse than this. But he would lose his strength; he wouldn't be able to get Mary out. He pulled at his bonds again. It was impossible to get his hands out of the leather straps.

He knew he'd have to wait and see how it turned out, and steeled himself for the ordeal.

Margate had untangled the old tools. They were simple in design. The cap was a band of steel that fitted around the victim's head at the temple. It could be tightened at four places to crush the skull. No good, Carter thought. It would render the victim unconscious too fast. It was the nut crusher he feared most. He could take the crushing of thumbnails, but the slow compressing of this testicles . . . that was a different matter entirely.

The big man wasn't in a hurry. He pulled up a chair and sat facing Carter with his back to Mary. He slipped the thumbscrews on Carter's hands with difficulty and started to apply pressure.

"Now. Who are you?" he asked calmly.

"You're a member of Parliament, I hear," Carter answered evenly. "Big man. Success in business." He grinned. Anything to distract the man, to get him mad and irrational.

"Who told you that? The guard that disappeared? Had to be. But he'd know very little."

"And you will find out nothing with these," Carter said, indicating the instruments with a sweep of his head.

Margate tightened the screws. The pain increased, but it wasn't unbearable. The nails had cracked and started to bleed. Carter willed himself, through yoga, not to feel the pain. But he heard something above the noise of Margate's voice and his own heavy breathing. What was it. Mary? She was struggling hard to free herself.

"It doesn't matter if you know who I am," Margate said. "Tomorrow you will be dead. One of our people is flying in to ask you some questions."

" 'Our people,' " Carter repeated. "My guess is you're a mole. Started very young. Patient. Gradually became powerful and influential."

Margate gave the screws another half turn. "Go on," he said. "You're doing well so far." He was scowling, totally absorbed with Carter.

"I can never figure out how you fellows maintain your loyalty," Carter said, trying to talk and keep control of the pain that streaked up his arms. "All those years of freedom, riches, power. And you're still loyal to a system that will take it away from you when you're no longer useful."

"It doesn't work that way," Margate said, in control again and smiling. He reached for the nut crushers and started to arrange them to encircle Carter's most precious possessions. He was fully absorbed, bent over, all his attention on the delicate task.

Carter had heard sounds from Mary's chair, but now they had stopped. He tried to look over Margate's shoulder to see what she was doing. As the big man bent lower, the luxuriant head of hair almost at Carter's chest, the man from AXE saw her chair. It was empty.

He looked around as the cold metal was attached to him and the screws were tightened. He couldn't see her.

Margate finally had the device attached to Carter's

testicles. As the first pain hit him, a pain that grew from his loins and traveled to his gut, he saw a chair circle from out of the gloom into the small area of light. It arced smoothly around from behind the grinning torturer. It struck Margate across the shoulders, the seat breaking in two over the back of his head.

Margate disappeared from his sight. In his place, Mary squatted in front of him, loosed the obscene instrument from his genitals and gently took off the thumbscrews. She slipped the leather straps from his arms and the rope from his ankles.

Carter didn't waste time with words. Those would come later. He tied the unconscious man, stuffed his mouth with rope, and took the woman by the arm. They walked out of the circle of light to the next room. As they found their night vision again, they saw a long set of wooden stairs against the far wall.

"We don't talk until this is over and we're out of here," Carter whispered. He led her up the stairs and to the heavy door at the top.

The huge room was dimly lit, and as far as Carter could see, deserted. He opted to move along one wall, under an overhang, away from the front door. At the far end of the room he found three doors.

He carefully opened the first. The room was dark. It was large, with a board room table in the middle and a huge desk at one end.

"Search every shelf and drawer for our clothes and my weapons," he whispered. He searched the desk while she concentrated on the shelves.

In the middle of the search, the door opened and a guard looked in, shined a flashlight once around the room, casually, and closed the door. Carter had sweated it out behind the huge desk. Mary had been lucky. She had less cover, but the light had missed her.

They came together after the search. "Nothing," Carter mouthed.

He headed for a door at the end of the office and peered inside. It was a small room, more like a secretary's office. He went for the desk while Mary opened a closet door. As he was about to open drawers, she called to him.

She had found their clothes. Her robe was ripped and soiled. His black fatigues weren't in much better shape, but they were welcome. In seconds they were dressed. Even their footwear was there.

"Wait a minute. I want to try the desk," Carter whispered, his face close to her ear. This was no time to make a stupid mistake.

The desk was a model of neatness. Every drawer held folders and office materials, all arranged with care. Carter felt beneath the contents of each drawer. He was about to give up, when his fingers found the softness of leather. Hugo's chamois sleeve. He drew out the razor-sharp stiletto with loving care. He breathed a sigh of relief as his hands found Wilhelmina and Pierre. He checked the Luger's load, slipped it and the little gas bomb in a pocket, and strapped on the stiletto. No matter what came next, he now felt ready for anything.

But a fight was not what he wanted. He had to get Mary out of there and find out what Hawk had learned.

The small room had one window. Carter examined it carefully for alarm systems and found none. The window opened to a grassy area at the back of the house.

Just as he was about to signal Mary to follow, the door opened and a large man in a business suit entered. He was reaching for a gun when Hugo found him. Carter had whipped out the stiletto and tossed it across the space between them.

He raced across the room, pulled the blade from Johnson's throat, and wiped it clean on his suit.

Mary stood stock-still and stared in horror. "He would have killed us both," Carter explained as he led her to the window. He signaled for Mary to follow and dropped to the ground. They waited, close together, their breathing almost nonexistent as they sought out the sounds of the night.

Nothing. No guards were in sight. No one had given an alarm.

They crept the full length of the house, keeping to the wall, under the overhanging eaves. Only an expanse of lawn separated them from the wall and escape.

The moon was behind clouds, but the earliest hint of dawn showed in the east. They crept to the wall without incident. Carter boosted Mary to the top. She had a foothold. He had just released her weight from his shoulders when he heard it.

The swift padding of canine feet . . . the intake and expelling of breath as lungs worked overtime . . . the deep growl at the bottom of a throat pulsing for the kill . . . the mouth alive with sharp white teeth, weapons designed to tear at flesh and crush bone.

Carter whirled and took three paces forward as the dog, a mastiff weighing at least a hundred pounds, came at him. The man from AXE, trained for every fight, fell backward with the dog's charge, grasped one paw, and catapulted the dog against the wall. He flipped to his feet and slipped out Hugo for the next charge. But no charge came. The dog's neck had been broken on impact with the wall.

Carter looked down on the animal with regret. The creature had been trained by man to kill. It had no choice. It deserved a better fate.

With a last look at the glazed eyes and the long tongue

lolling from its open mouth, Carter vaulted the wall and joined Mary on the other side.

The old boat touched the side of the boathouse as full dawn lit the eastern sky. Carter led Mary Wyness to her house, gathered his belongings while she packed a bag, and drove her to the pub.

For the second time that morning, Carter knocked on the back door. Brodie let them in without comment. He and his wife Maggie were at breakfast, a loaf of crusty bread and a large wedge of cheese between them on a wood cutting board. Two bowls with the remains of oatmeal had been pushed to one side.

"Come in," he said, indicating chairs for them. "What's Mary Wyness got to do with this?" he asked. "What the hell happened to her face?"

Maggie Brodie got up to pour two more mugs of tea and cut some bread and cheese. She kept her mouth firmly shut.

Carter was reluctant to go into it, but he'd already gone too far with the locals. There was no point in holding back now. "They took her captive to get me," he said. "She was a tigress. Saved us both." He looked at her as he raised the steaming mug. "Thanks," he said.

She raised a mug to him in salute, saying nothing.

"I'll have some of that cheese and bread, but may I make a call first?" he asked.

"Sure," Brodie said, leading the way to the front of the pub and a phone behind the bar. "After your call, I want to know it all. You're not the only one at risk here."

Carter nodded and picked up the phone. He dialed in the codes that would take him through to the AXE computer, then gave his N3 code and another three digits to get through to Hawk . . . an emergency code.

"What's happening, Nick?" the gruff voice of the head of AXE asked without preamble.

While he hated to hold back from his chief, Carter wasn't about to tell him about the rescue. "Nothing at this end. I called to get instructions. Do we have political problems?"

"Right as usual. They're sure who's behind it, but they can't make up their minds to move."

"What do you want me to do?"

"Stay out of the area. Go back to London. Call me every couple of days or let Cynthia know where you are at all times."

"Do we get first crack at them when the decision comes down?"

"I got that promise. It's very big, Nick. Could be the biggest intelligence coup in a decade. I don't know why they're delaying. Probably scared of finding the truth and scared not to clean out the rot. Just keep in touch," the older man said. He sounded tired. It would be about two in the morning in Washington.

After the call, Carter returned to the kitchen. He ate some cheese and a couple of pieces of bread. During the meal little was said. Carter lit a cigarette and broke the silence.

"I'm taking Mary out of here. I don't know where yet."

"I've got some friends in Aberdeen," she said.

"Good. I'm taking her to Aberdeen. Then I'm off to London. I'll probably be back in a few days." He looked from Brodie to his wife. "I hope you won't be foolish. No matter what happens, let Sergeant Penny handle it. Tell all the others to keep clear. Promise?"

"If you say so," Jack Brodie said. "But they're going to want to know more. They've got nothing to do but be curious. What the hell do I tell them?"

"Jesus," Carter exclaimed. "I don't want them involved in this. Don't tell them about Mary. Mrs. Brodie"—he looked her straight in the eye—"if the women ask, Mary's just gone to Aberdeen for a few days. Okay?"

Maggie Brodie, the biggest gossip in Poolewe, just nodded and said nothing.

"One last thing," Carter said. "They may use a scapegoat. Just go along with it."

"I don't know what you mean," Brodie said.

"Penny may be ordered to find a drifter and shoot him in the act of escaping . . . something like that."

"Christ! Penny may be an ass, but he'd never do anything like that," Brodie protested.

"They could provide the body and force Penny to go along. Don't forget, they've got him in pretty deep already."

"Hard to believe," Brodie muttered, shaking his head.

"I only said it's possible. Just tell the boys not to do anything. Promise?"

"Sure," Brodie said as Carter and Mary got up to leave. "I promise."

Maggie Brodie just watched in silence.

SEVEN

Carter's flight from Aberdeen arrived at Heathrow a few minutes before midnight. He'd thought about Cynthia on the way down and was looking forward to seeing her. She made no demands, always seemed ready to sit and talk about their work or soothe his tired psyche with the softness of her body.

The fastest way to London wasn't by cab. So Carter followed the relatively thin flow of humanity down to the bowels of the terminal to the tube station and took the Piccadilly Line into the heart of London.

The walls of the long escalators were covered with advertisements for products, West End shows, and even politicians. Between the framed messages, graffiti swirls in every color filled the empty spaces as far as the arm could reach.

Later, the few faces around him blurred as the car rushed through the underground tunnel. His mind turned to Mary Wyness and the events at Poolewe. He'd dropped Mary at her friends' home in Aberdeen, then rushed for Dyce Airport to barely make the ten o'clock flight. The face of old Jack Brodie kept intruding on his thoughts as the car rushed on. Would the innkeeper and the others be smart enough to stay clear of it until he could bring the mystery to an end?

He lost track of time, and glanced up just as the name

of a station flashed by as the train picked up speed again: Leicester Square. His stop was next: Covent Garden. He stood, clutching his bag in one hand and his radio/tape deck in the other, and stepped onto the platform when the doors opened. Soon he was on the endless escalator to the street.

Covent Garden was a dark rectangle of glass and steel that blocked the cloudless sky. The opera house across the street was dark, its patrons long gone, home in bed. Carter ducked into the dark recesses of the theater's front door, and in the shadows, quickly removed his gun and knife from their hiding places in the radio. He slipped Hugo into its sheath and Wilhelmina into the holster he hadn't removed before boarding the place. The X-ray proof radio/recorder had been through customs and immigration with him at airports around the world.

Portsmouth Street and Cynthia's flat was just three blocks away. But it was a dangerous and dimly lit three blocks, and Carter's well-tuned senses were alert to every sound. As he crossed to the next block, he heard what he had been half expecting—the light shuffle of feet behind him. As the sound drew closer, two men stepped from an alley in front of him. Light reflected from the steel they carried—polished and sharpened.

Carter stopped, stooping quickly to put his bag and radio against a building. Hugo slid to his palm, the blade still hidden, and he turned with his back to a chalky red brick wall.

While he could see four of them in the dim light, he didn't feel fear. He'd been in this situation too many times. But a gang of four attacking one man? A fleeting thought skimmed through his brain. The enemy in Scotland? Had he been followed? No. This had to be coincidental.

But these four didn't look as if they wanted his wallet and a quiet chat. As the thought occurred, one lunged at him swinging his knife in a wide arc. Carter ducked to one side and down, Hugo flashing into view and out in one straight cutting motion. Carter's old friend pierced the man's arm and was out in a microsecond. The attacker screamed in pain as his knife clattered to the pavement and into dark shadows.

The other three closed in, more cautious than before but not willing to let a lone man get away.

A second man feinted to the left and lunged to his right, bringing his blade up from below in commando fashion.

Carter stepped slightly to one side, grasped his assailant's wrist in one hand, and twisted. As the man's arm was bent hard and the bone snapped, the stiletto slit the attacker's wrist. A second weapon skittered off into the gloom.

These four weren't going to give up. The first man had found his knife and had joined the fray using his other hand.

Now Carter faced three of them again. He drew Wilhelmina.

The three backed off but didn't flee. What the hell was the matter with them? Carter wondered. He didn't want to fire. In the fight, he had moved away from the wall. The fourth man was out of his sight. Carter swiveled from left to right, sighting his gun, seeking the fourth man.

Too late, he saw the upraised arm, the flash of steel as the man poised for the throw. As his arm came down and Carter's gun turned too late, a second blade flashed through the air and plunged into the thrower's shoulder.

The man grunted but didn't go down. Instead he melted into the darkness. When Carter turned to face the other three, they had gone. This was their territory and they knew every alley and doorway.

"It's a sad day when the famous Killmaster can't defend himself against some of my less fortunate neighbors," a laughing voice said as its owner stepped from the darkness. Cynthia Talbot was wearing a clinging nightgown of thin material and nothing else.

"How . . . ?"

"I was having a last smoke and looked out the window. That bastard took my best throwing knife with him. You owe me one."

She came to him and clung, laughing as she fixed her mouth on his and probed with her tongue. "A good fight makes me horny as hell," she said at last. "That wasn't much of a fight, but it will have to do. Come on," she chuckled. "I've got a warm bed waiting."

When the door closed behind them, Cynthia wriggled out of her nightgown and sprawled on the bed. She waited for him to put down his bags and take off his clothes.

Carter was as ready as she. But he moved deliberately, put down his bag and the radio, slipped off his gun and knife. He sat on the bed, pulled off one shoe and then the other, slowly, tantalizingly, playing the game he knew would infuriate her. When she was maddened by his delays, her juices flowed all the more.

Finally she ran out of patience, growled at him with mock ferocity, and flew at him.

He fell back on the bed, laughing.

She kissed him hard on the mouth, forcing her tongue deep between his teeth. She rubbed her breasts against his chest. Then, in a lightning move, she jumped from him, caught the bottom of his pants, and pulled.

Carter lay back on the bed again, grinning, with only his unbuttoned shirt left, when she attacked once more. She sought his mouth, panting hard. As she forced open his lips with her tongue, she tugged at the shirt with one hand, pulling it from his arms.

Carter was aroused enough for anything, but she wasn't ready for the finale yet. She moved down his chest, kissing as she moved. Her mouth encircled him, drawing on him insistently until he felt the center of his being drawn out by a soft and sensuous vacuum.

She chose that exact moment to release her prisoner from the depths of her throat. He had started to regain some control, when she moved up on him quickly, positioned herself above him, and slid back and forth until, with a new gentleness, she admitted him.

Slowly, she moved with him, letting his length penetrate until they were fully joined, her belly against his.

She continued to move over him. The languid pace was agonizing. The ecstasy of the long, drawn-out movements to and fro was more than he could stand. He took her full weight in his arms, the long, delicious length of her, turned her over to rest beneath him without disturbing their rhythm, and applied more pressure as her legs parted to admit him even deeper.

It was his turn to move slowly, but not as slowly as she. The motion quickened as they moved as one. Sweat provided a lubricant for every inch of their skin. The man-woman smell of them attacked their senses.

They moved more rapidly . . . with more urgency.

The sensual motion of flesh on flesh had been maddening, had taken them up the slope, but the surge of feeling, of rapturous sensation, attacked every cell of their bodies, carrying them to a crest.

They hung there, suspended, not wanting to go over the top, afraid that more sensation would bring pain instead of pleasure.

The scale tipped, their wanting adding weight, their need taking them over a crest to a new plateau. Then they climbed another slope, higher than the first, the sound of skin slapping on skin, echoing their ragged breathing.

Then the world burst like an exploding sun. It came apart and flowed over them like a giant wave, all-engulfing, bringing pain and pleasure both. He stayed on her for long minutes, then slid to the sheet to fold himself close to her as she clung to him.

The heaving of their chests gradually stopped as lungs and hearts returned to normal. Their damp hair rested on a pillow as they lay unspeaking. It had always been good with them, but it had never been like this. They both knew it and were happy just to lie there, touching, thinking, and remembering.

Minutes passed, but both were unwilling to move and break the spell. Even the lure of a cigarette didn't tempt Carter.

Then a bell rang shrilly not far from their ears. Neither moved.

"It's the AXE line," Cynthia groaned, and she rolled from him. "We've got to answer it."

She reached out a slim arm and brought the offending instrument to her ear. She listened.

"It's Hawk," was all she said as she handed over the phone.

"I called at a bad time?" the older man said.

"Just came in the door," Carter said. It was the third time that week he'd been less than honest with his mentor, and he didn't like it. He knew he could never let it become a habit. But this was really just a little white lie.

"The information came a lot sooner than I expected."

"And the permission? It's our job?" Carter asked.

"Your job, Nick."

"How far do I go?"

"All the way. They want the installation totally destroyed and the principals with it."

"Tell me about the main man," Carter said, imagining the Englishman the way he'd seen him at his Scottish home.

"You were right. He's a member of Parliament, highly respected, a wealthy businessman, very powerful and influential. Geremy Farnsworth Margate."

"What do they give as a description?" Carter asked, wanting to match that information with the man he'd seen.

"He's tall, slightly overweight, has a full head of gray hair. He's got the ruddy complexion of an English country gentleman, blue eyes, crow's feet. He has the bearing and self-confidence of a very successful man."

"What did we pick up on his background?" Carter asked, conscious of Cynthia listening at his ear.

"Too many scenarios. A lot of guesses," Hawk said, his words partly garbled by the stub of his cigar. "But there's one guess that fascinates me. They've traced him back to his parents or pseudoparents. Their history goes back as far as World War Two, but it's pretty hazy before that. I think the bastard's been a mole for more than forty years."

"Christ! Who were his parents?"

"His father claimed to be a naval hero who lost his leg in the war and settled—and get this," he emphasized, "they settled at Poolewe back in the early forties."

"Sounds like a classic Soviet plot," Carter said.

"Early KGB or pre-KGB," Hawk offered. "Anyway,

they were financed and built up an extensive clothing business. Young Geremy went to the best schools, developed all the best contacts. He's as solid in the old boy network over there as you can get. You know how much that means in England.''

''He couldn't have been more than eight or ten,'' Carter said.

''My guess would be closer to eight. What I can't figure is risking him in something as tenuous as this. Those underground pens had to be found sooner or later. The Russians are neither careless nor stupid. Something doesn't wash.''

''Let's be thankful for all the help we can get,'' Carter said. ''If the other side didn't make mistakes, we'd both be singing with the angels.''

''More probably stoking the furnaces of hell, Nick,'' Hawk said and chuckled. ''Be careful, but destroy the bastard. The P.M. was definite on that. Margate has to be destroyed when the whole thing goes up. I don't care how you do it, but destroy them all. No identification of Margate can ever get out.''

''What about family?'' Cynthia whispered.

Carter repeated the question.

''That's my job. When it's over, MI5 will work with me on the cleanup.''

''All right. I'll fly up today. Cynthia's people will supply explosives and a chopper. I may need a lot of gear.''

''I don't want to know the details. Keep me posted on your progress,'' Hawk said, hanging up abruptly.

Cynthia rolled over on her back and stared at the ceiling as Carter hung up. ''He's always been a curt old bastard,'' she said.

''That's just his way. Hawk doesn't like to show his

feelings. He's lost too many people through the years.''

They lay in silence for a while, each involved in separate thoughts.

Finally Carter spoke. "I'll need a couple of dozen timers, the same number of detonators and a few pounds of plastic explosives. Try for C4 if you can get it," he said, thinking ahead to the final showdown. "Throw in a couple of machine pistols, a flack jacket, and a few pairs of dark fatigues. Make sure it's for night fighting. This could be a commando job."

"No problem. I've got most of it, and I'll fly you up in a chopper."

"I'll need scuba gear as well. Extra tanks and a couple of wet suits."

"Where will you stay this time?"

"I've got a deserted farm spotted. On the coast, but away from the action. You fly me in at night and come straight back here."

"No way. I'm in this from here on."

"Sorry, luv. You've got a station to help run and that's it."

"We'll see, Mr. Carter. We'll see."

EIGHT

Carter had always had his own pied-à-terre in London, an old hotel on Sloane Square called the Royal Court. He was known there, always had the same room overlooking the square. It was a dangerous indulgence for a man in his profession but a weakness he didn't want to change. He wasn't known as Nick Carter there. He was an American weapons salesman, James Long.

Carter may have gone to some lengths for privacy, but he was never careless about his identity or his actions. He never went to or from the Royal Court without checking for a tail, doubling back on his tracks, changing cabs and tube lines. If anyone found him there, it would have to be an accident, or a hell of a piece of sleuthing. Cynthia didn't know about his hideout, though she had tried to find it. Only Hawk knew about it.

That was why Carter was puzzled when two men accosted him by name when he was sitting in the private bar enjoying an evening drink alone. The bar was off the lobby to the left, small and cozy. When the hotel had been remodeled in 1982, the decor had been left much the same, old wood and leather. The same bartender, Sam, had been there since the year one. While the public bar was large, filled and noisy, the one he used never contained more than a half-dozen guests.

The two men slipped into seats opposite him. One lit a

cigarette and stared at Carter for a few seconds before he spoke.

"We are from the British government. No names. No identification. Just a message," he said. He was hatless, wore a well-tailored gray striped suit. He was blond, tall and muscular. Carter pegged him as either Scotland Yard, CID, or MI5.

"One of our members of Parliament has lodged a complaint about you. We don't appreciate our people being harassed by foreign agencies," the other one said. He had a face like carved rock, blunt and squared-off. His hair was dark, his eyes as black as a starless night, his hands gnarled blocks of wood. They matched the size of him. Sitting opposite Carter he blocked out one end of the room. He had to be like the other—from one of the internal services of the British intelligence machine.

Carter grinned. He couldn't be mad at these two. The three of them were too much alike. But he had a job to do and Hawk had assured him MI5 was going to be working with him.

"My work is already cleared with the head man at MI5," he said. Then he realized he might have gone too far. Suppose Margate had some of them in his pocket—literally. It was possible. But sometimes you had to trust your instincts. This time he did. And his instincts told him they were the real thing, and probably on the level.

He had to respect their ability. They had found him when others couldn't. They may not have known exactly who he was, but they knew he was from an American agency. It was enough. It was too much. Farewell to the Royal Court, fond memories of peaceful evenings and the friends he'd made at Sloane Square.

"What the hell does that mean?" the big one asked,

his voice like a foghorn even though he was trying to keep it down.

"It means we all have weaknesses. We make mistakes. Communications break down," Carter said, picking up his pack of cigarettes and his lighter, lighting one without offering them around. He blew smoke over their heads as he went on. "Within your organization some people know some things others don't. My chief is working with the head of MI5. That's all you have to know. Now, get off my ass," Carter said flatly.

They looked at each other. The smaller one nodded. They rose and left without another word.

Ten minutes later, his bag packed, the bill paid, Carter was on a computer communications connection to Hawk. He had already told him about the two, given complete descriptions, down to the bitten fingernails, tobacco-stained fingers, an acne-scarred face. "I'm checking out. I'll let you know when I select another hotel," he told Hawk.

"What's next on the agenda?"

"Nothing you don't know. Back to Scotland tonight. Cynthia has all the tools I need and transport. I meet her in a couple of hours."

"Keep me informed," Hawk said, hanging up without further comment.

Cynthia had never been an orthodox agent following orders to the letter, and she wasn't an orthodox assistant chief of station. She used the worldwide resources of Amalgamated Press and Wire Services, the cover organization for AXE, and she used AXE to its fullest, but she always had to have her own little network, one that could work outside officialdom and Hawk's strict orders. Carter had run into it before. It was one thing that drew him to her. He also knew that Hawk was aware of her occasional detours and that the canny old warrior turned a blind eye.

So, true to form, the chopper she produced was a beat-up old Huey an ex-Vietnam contact of hers had overhauled for local hire. It was gunmetal gray, the paint inside chipped, the shine of bare metal showing where dog soldiers and chopper crews had sat through the hours of hell on patrol. It still had the mounts for the big 60mm's that had scythed down Viet Cong and ravaged their emplacements.

Cynthia had hired the pilot to take them in. His name was Jake Malone, a former soldier of fortune now down on his luck. He was the product of an American mother and a Scottish father. He had settled in England after the Vietnam War. A man disillusioned with the States, he had sought a better life in England and hadn't found it.

"Jake, this is Nick Carter. Nick, Jake Malone," she said, making the introductions.

"Another of your spooks?" Malone asked.

"No questions, Jake," she told the overweight pilot. "You fly us in and you get the hell out. That's it."

Carter threw the gear Cynthia had collected into the back of the ancient machine and climbed in. He tried to close the sliding side doors, but the runners had long ago been squashed and the doors remained permanently open. It was going to be a cold and noisy ride.

When they were airborne between London and Birmingham, Carter pulled the headphones off Cynthia and shouted into her ear over the racket, "You aren't going to do more than help unload. It's back to London for you, luv."

"No way. I'm part of this now."

"Sorry. You're out. That's it."

He watched as she sulked for a few seconds, then felt

uneasy as she shrugged, smiled to herself, and pulled on the earphones.

They took two hours to get to Carlisle, north of the Lake District, where Malone put down to refuel at a small airport. People like Jake Malone operated in a separate society, among people of like kind who knew the secret places, the out-of-the-way fueling stops, all the ways to avoid contact with the real world.

Carter jumped to the ground, flexed his cramped thigh muscles, and rummaged through his kit for a windbreaker. The sky was overcast. They had been flying at relatively low altitude with moist cold air blasting at them. He thought about the countless times he'd landed in remote places on the way to a job, on assignment to eliminate some other Geremy Margate. He thought about his brief talk with Mary Wyness, a displaced person. He wondered if she'd ever find herself. Perhaps the hours she'd been captive would help her to shake the lethargy that had made her a prisoner of Poolewe.

He shut out the random thoughts. Too much time for thinking. Too much time getting from here to there. Too many hours to think about what he'd done with his life. Carter knew he wasn't really alive unless he was in action. But he was also closer to death then. Sometimes he thought about the laws of probability. They told him he couldn't get away forever with all the close calls he'd had. His skills, like a gambler's, shaped the odds to favor him. But they were still odds—never a certainty.

Malone had climbed into the cockpit and Cynthia was sitting beside him. Carter pulled himself up and swung aboard. Next stop: Scotland.

The farmhouse and barn had been deserted for years. Most of the windows had been shattered by flying debris caught up by onshore breezes. It was on a lonely point three miles from Poolewe on the rocky cliffs looking down on Loch Ewe. A mile from the local road, it would serve for the time.

They came in from the sea, all riding lights off, and set down as quietly as possible next to the house. Cynthia helped Carter unload and started for the house. He caught her by the arm, lifted her, and tossed her aboard, her rump taking a beating on the riveted steel floor.

Carter signaled to Malone over the noise of the slowly rotating blades, then watched as the old crate lifted off. As agreed, it headed out to sea on the first leg of its flight, the noise of its going lost in the constant crashing of the angry sea against rock.

He stood and watched them disappear. The black night claimed the aircraft and left him alone. He stood, listening to the sea sounds, breathing in the salt air and a faint smell of rotted fish. Then he broke the spell and turned to the pile of supplies.

Carter lugged all the gear inside. After blacking out the few unbroken windows facing inland, he lit a propane lamp Cynthia had provided. The smell of gas, at initial lighting, blocked out the smell of dampness for the moment.

As usual, Cynthia had been efficient. She had substituted two Walther machine pistols, each with a Larand sound suppressor, for the Uzis he preferred. They were thirty shot, 9mm, and were still in their paper wrapping, oiled and ready. He doubted if he'd use one of the pair of Beretta 92S handguns she'd provided. But they also had Larands affixed and they might be better in the cavern: with his Luger's sharp bark, it might not be the ideal weapon if he took the cammando approach.

She had also provided Kevlar vests. They were the newest development designed to be worn over battle dress, buttoned under the groin to protect your ass and other vital parts. These had webbing attached for grenades, commando knives, water bottles, and a full backpack if needed. They had pouches on each hip for explosives. Cynthia had supplied extra clips, boxes of ammo, knitted stevedore hats, blackface make-up—everything in black, dulled metal. Even the sneakers she'd supplied were black. And everything paired up. One in large size and one in small.

He grinned. She was a stubborn woman.

Other boxes contained C4, each pound of plastic explosive rolled like a sausage two inches thick and four inches long. As he thought about his tactics, he rolled the sausages into tennis-ball-size globes and plugged a detonator into each. The balls he would put in one pouch, the timers she had supplied in the other. A half dozen would be enough for the raid he had planned.

Last, he unwrapped a double-edged commando knife. It felt strange in his hand, so much larger than Hugo. The knife alone was enough to make him feel vaguely foolish, a Rambo-like pretend soldier.

He stripped to his underwear, pulled on a set of black fatigues, looked at his faithful Luger, and laid it aside. He slipped into one of the Kevlar vests, filled the pouches with plastic and timers, pushed extra clips into webbing slots, and, reluctantly, holstered a Beretta. Hugo was set beside Wilhelmina, but Pierre was still taped to his inner thigh. He reached through a slot in the vest to make sure he could get at the small gas bomb, then sat down to darken his face. With a knitted black cap to complete the outfit, he looked like something out of *Soldier of Fortune* magazine. Glancing in a grimy mirror on the kitchen wall, he almost laughed. He slung one of the Walthers over his shoulder and started for the door. Then he turned back. The commando knife was still sitting on a box, big, reflecting the light. He picked it up, hefted it again, and slipped it into a scabbard in the webbing.

Carter turned down the lamp and headed for the door. Again he stopped, picked up his old friends, complete with the familiar leather holster and the chamois sheath, wrapped them in the paper he'd discarded from the Walther, and hid them under a broken section of the floor. The rest of Cynthia's toys he left in their boxes.

Carter trotted at a swift pace toward the town, the Walther held across his chest at the ready. It took him fifteen minutes to reach Jock Fraser's house. He looked at his Rolex. It was fifteen minute after closing at the pub. The house was dark. He squatted in the dark and waited.

In a half hour, a half-drunk Jock Fraser came by, singing to himself as he ambled slowly down the deserted street. The Scotsman crossed his front lawn and reached for the unlocked door. One powerful hand closed over his mouth while the other circled his chest, holding him still.

"Jock. It's Nick. Don't make any noise. We have to talk," Carter said.

The Scotsman relaxed and was released. He turned around and gasped involuntarily. "Jesus save us!" he said.

Carter knew he must have looked like a monster, a mercenary from hell.

"What the hell are you dressed up for?" Fraser blurted out.

"Never mind. It's all part of the problem. I need your help. The boat again, and an old truck if you have one." He reached into an inner pocket and took out a wad of bills.

"Put that back. I've already got more of your money than the boat is worth. You're welcome to whatever I've got."

"I'm taking the boat now. What about the vehicle?"

"An old truck. A small Bedford. It'll be in the driveway here in an hour."

"Good enough. Did you manage to keep the boys from doing anything foolish?"

"Some of them are talking about a private war. They didn't think you were coming back."

Carter looked at the smaller man, his features severe. "I may not be able to go back again—to sit with you for a pint. I'm committed and they know me. So whatever you do, you have to keep the boys out of it. Tell them this is my job. Talk to Jack Brodie. He's got a level head. He'll talk to them too."

Fraser stood in the yard, the devil who stood like a man standing in front of him. He threw up his hands. "I'll do what I can. They're the most stubborn bunch of jackasses you're ever likely to meet."

He turned to say something else, but he was talking to himself. He looked down to the boathouse and saw the doors ajar. The diesel started up and then purred as the boat was backed out.

He stood looking at the black boat and the man in black in wonder, barely able to see them.

"God help us," he said aloud as he walked to the house.

NINE

The chop was light. Cloud cover darkened the rock face at the entrance to the cavern. Unlike his first trip, when Carter had faced only a bored sentry, two men patrolled the entrance, alert, their backs straight, their automatic rifles at the ready.

The Killmaster felt like Rambo in blackface as he rounded a rocky outcropping. He was assuming only part of that role. He was licensed to kill, but he wasn't a wholesale killer. It wasn't his intent to spray the entire complement of guards with lead and leave them piled up like cordwood.

He had the Walther set at single fire. It coughed twice, the sound lost in the crash of seawater on rock. The two guards went down, each with a shattered shoulder, their weapons clattering against rock and sliding into the wea. Carter paused to tie their legs and arms and leave them propped against the rock wall.

The interior of the cavern was larger than he'd imagined. Beyond the first three submarines he'd seen on his second visit, the hollowed-out space nature had provided stretched back as far as he could see. The roof varied from two hundred to two hundred and fifty feet.

Strings of naked light bulbs hung overhead in no set pattern. Near the entrance they were strung sparsely, but farther in, where most of the work was in progress, they were more frequent, supplemented by scores of fluorescents.

The waterway was narrow at the entrance, allowing only one sub to exit. Their engineers couldn't change this feature without bringing down tons of rock and enlarging the entrance. For the length of two subs within the entrance, the breadth of the waterway widened to twice the size. A hundred yards inside the cavern a huge pool, almost like a small lake, could accommodate five subs abreast with room to spare.

The place was immense.

Carter could see men working on the steel-hulled sea monsters. They scrambled over the superstructures, some welding steel plates, some placing plexiglass over the control room observation areas, some working massive cranes that loaded the fighting ships with weapons and supplies.

The smell of diesel fumes from the cranes was sharp and biting, but not uncomfortable. They had to have massive fans somewhere for ventilation. Carter made a note to find and destroy them.

Men in olive uniforms patrolled the whole area. They were all men with Slavic features, big men, well muscled. They all carried AK-47s, the Finnish versions, the same as Carter had seen in the hands of the guard he'd questioned earlier.

To one side, on a shelf of rock that was not a part of the waterway, Carter came to a dry dock that held two subs. He could see that the docking areas were cut from the steel of the original oil storage tanks. It must have been one hell of a job to cut them up and get rid of all the scrap steel. They were upright, supported by timber braces. No one was working on them.

But this wasn't getting the job done. He reached for a ball of C4, molded it behind one of the supports close to a sub's superstructure, and slipped on the timing device. He set it for four hours. Then he checked his watch. It was ten minutes to one in the morning. He pulled out the other timers, one at a time, and set them all to blow at exactly 4:50.

As he turned to seek other locations to place explosives, a uniformed man was leveling his automatic rifle, clicking off the safety. Sweat started to break out on Carter's brow as his hand flashed for Wilhelmina, a habit that went back for years. Too late, he realized she wasn't there. As he reached for the silenced Beretta, he could see the man's finger squeeze the trigger. Carter braced himself for a hail of lead. At the same instant the Beretta coughed once, the man's gun jammed and he went over backward, a neat hole in the center of his forehead.

Carter pulled the body behind the sub and slipped the man's rifle into the water. The Killmaster had been lucky. They'd issued this guard an old Kalashnikov, Russian-made. The Russian models had been notoriously bad.

He looked around. Nothing of the dead guard or the fight was obvious. He turned toward a wooden shack he'd seen closer to the back of the cavern, avoiding other men in olive-drab who patrolled everywhere. He skirted them, one at a time, his image, all in black, blending with the dark colors around him.

The shack was twenty feet by ten. Crudely built, it looked out of place. A hasp on the door held it shut. An open padlock was draped over the hasp. Carter lifted the padlock and pulled the door open slowly, making sure the rusted hinges didn't reveal his presence. He needn't have worried. The sounds of the giant cranes, the constant welding, and the ring of steel hammers on steel hulls hid any noise he made.

He had some luck at last. The shack was stacked with explosives for further excavation, boxes of ammunition, primers. They were enough to blow the roof off the cavern and destroy everything in it.

He moved inside, took two balls of plastic explosive from a pouch, removed one of the primers, and molded them into one. He separated two wooden crates of TNT, placed the plastic between them, and slipped on the timer, already set for four hours. It was ten minutes after one now. Three hours and forty minutes from zero hour.

Carter stepped out of the shack, replaced the padlock, and melded with the wall of rock, waiting for a patrol of guards to pass. He thought of his orders. Margate had to go. He had to be a part of the destruction and his name was never to be linked with the project. That was easier said than done. He was going to take the best shot he had and nail Margate later if he had to.

He had another problem. The mass killing. He didn't want the men working here to be blown with his bombs. He'd have to find some last-minute way to warn them to get out. First, he had to finish the job and get the hell out himself.

He craned to see past the shack. The way was clear. Carter drifted along the rock wall, moving upward with every step, making for the top and the ventilators. Halfway up, he came to another wooden structure, cantilevered against the rock. From the glass windows all along its front wall, one would be able to see the whole work area below. He assumed it was the engineering office. He stopped at the bottom of the structure supporting it, molded a ball of plastic against one huge beam, and slipped on a timer. It was half past one. Zero hour was less three hours and twenty minutes.

Closer to the top, Carter could hear the noise of the fans acting as ventilators. Above their steady hum, the throb of two huge diesels was almost overpowering. Two giant generators, diesel-powered, were supplying electricity to the cavern. As he listened, one shut down to become backup for the other. Quickly, as guards patrolled below, Carter placed a charge between the two generators. When this one went, everything would shut down whether or not the other charges blew.

He had one ball of C4 left and he intended to use it on the ventilators or the entrance doors at the surface. As he started to rise from his crouched position, he heard the bark of an AK-47 from behind. The slugs hit him in the kidneys and the rib cage, and finally a glancing shot to the side of his head. They were like hammer blows in the hands of a powerful man. They threw him against the wall in front of him. He bounced off the rock surface and lay on the stone floor. He slowly felt the lights go out.

It was ten minutes to two. A hundred and eighty minutes to zero hour.

Carter opened his eyes. A naked bulb of high wattage blinded him. He couldn't see beyond it.

He listened. Nothing stirred in the room, or wherever he was. He hurt all over. His head was bandaged. A gong went off in his brain every few seconds. He tried to examine himself carefully, but his wrists and ankles were secured with rope.

He'd blown it.

They had stripped him of his weapons and his flack jacket. Thank God for the Kevlar, or thank Cynthia. Most of the slugs had hit the vest. One had grazed his temple. He was still dressed in the black fatigues.

Carter had no way of knowing if Pierre was still with

him. Probably not. They would have patted him down carefully. He tried to focus his mind on his upper thigh, but he couldn't tell if the tape was there or not.

A door opened and he heard the scuffle of feet. Two. No, three pairs. One a boot, military; the other two civilian, softer leather. A box of supplies separated him from them. He couldn't see who they were.

"He was kneeling between the two generators when one of my men shot him. We thought you'd want to question him," the military man said in Russian.

"Good work, as far as it went," a high-pitched voice said sarcastically.

"What do you mean, Comrade Gregarov? My man did well."

"What was the intruder doing kneeling at the generators? Have you searched?" another voice joined in. This one was calmer, deeper.

"My men are doing that now. He had some plastic explosives in a pouch. The timer was set to blow at ten minutes to five," the military man said.

"What?" the high-pitched voice cried. "What time is it now?"

"Twenty minutes after four, Comrade Gregarov."

"That's only a half hour!" Gregarov shouted.

Christ! He'd been out for more than two hours, Carter thought. Too long. He'd never be in top form when he needed to be.

He craned his head around the box. He could see all three pairs of footwear now. The military man wore boots, solid and well kept. The complainer wore scuffed oxfords, cheap and needing new heels. The third man wore Western-style boots of fine leather, polished and elegant.

The door opened and a fourth man entered. Carter

could see his shoes, Italian loafers, highly polished and expensive.

"What's going on here?" the newcomer demanded. "I've just arrived and I hear about a bomb threat."

"Who are you?" Gregarov demanded.

"I'm Colonel Kisigin. Comrade Margate asked Moscow for help," the newcomer said imperiously. "Now I shall repeat your question. Just who the hell are *you*?"

"I'm Yuri Gregarov, in charge of this project. When Comrade Margate is absent, I am in control," he said, equally imperiously.

"A scientist," Kisigin said with a sneer. "That explains the chaos I saw on the way in. Where is Margate?"

"He had to return to London, Colonel," Berof said calmly.

"This is my assistant," Gregarov said offhandedly.

"I am Colonel Valeri Berof. First Chief Directorate. Third Department," he said calmly.

"You didn't tell me . . . they didn't say . . . you're KGB!" Gregarov gasped.

Carter wiggled to see more. Kisigin, a tall man, thin and bald, with hawklike features, held out his hand to Berof. "Good to find someone of competence here, Colonel."

"The Third Department includes the United Kingdom. I wanted to see this operation firsthand. And I wanted to observe Margate. He's been away from the motherland a long time."

"But you're a scientist," Gregarov moaned.

"I am many things, comrade," Berof said softly.

"Perhaps Margate has been here too long," Kisigin agreed, ignoring Gregarov. "Your reasons are my reasons, Berof. When the request for someone to interrogate a prisoner came across my desk at Serbsky, I too felt it warranted a look from on high.'' He paused to look at the military man, a major. "I presume you are in charge of security here.''

Gregarov stared from one to the other, fear apparent in his face.

The military man saluted and held out a hand. "Major Anatole Lobanov, GRU. General Gorgalov, chief of the GRU, felt he should be represented.''

To hear the mention of GRU, military intelligence, was too much for Gregarov. He slumped in a chair.

"Good." Kisigin held out his hand. Then he frowned. "They told me when I arrived that my prisoner had escaped.''

"We have him again." Lobanov grinned broadly.

"Excellent." Kisigin grinned back.

Carter could see that the man took pleasure in his work. The colonel saw Carter's head sticking out from the other side of the crate. When he approached, his face registered cruelty. He pulled Carter across the room by the hair sticking out of the bandage, and to a chair under another bare bulb. The light shone in Carter's eyes from two feet away.

Gregarov sat in a chair nearby, a perturbed expression on his narrow face. He was dressed in a lab coat and reached for his cigarettes with yellowed fingers.

The KGB man had taken off his lab coat. He wore a neat gray suit underneath, was younger than Gregarov, a man of middle height and weight, pleasant-looking and assured.

Major Lobanov stood, scowling at Carter. He was a big man, bull-necked, double-chinned, red-complexioned. Carter had killed some of his men, had made a fool of him. He looked like a man who would be unforgiving.

"You will tell me what you are doing here," Kisigin said simply.

Carter knew this was the colonel's first line of questioning and it would get progressively worse. Well, the Russian was going to get a surprise. Carter had decided this was not the time to undergo pain or to be subject to drugs that would pickle his brain. Another day. Another battle. "I came to blow up your project," he said, just as simply.

He could see the colonel was taken back. He had come a long way to show off his skills only to have the victim fall at his feet at the first gentle prod.

A captain had come and gone during the last few seconds. He had whispered in the major's ear and left.

"He's not lying," Lobanov said. "My people have found the bomb," he beamed.

"Did you find other bombs on him?" Kisigin asked impatiently.

"One," the major said. "It was primed. He also had a timer set for ten minutes to five. The one we found was set for the same time."

Kisigin looked at his watch. "It's four-thirty," he said, his voice showing less confidence. "How many others did he set?"

"Oh, my God!" Gregarov moaned. "I am a scientist. I know nothing of this . . . this kind of thing. How did I get into this?"

"Because you design weapons to kill millions. You deserve to go first," Carter said, grinning.

Kisigin drew back his hand and slapped Carter as hard as he could. The Killmaster slewed around in the chair but didn't fall.

"Is that the best that comes out of the famous Serbsky Institute?" he goaded. "By my guess, we have less than fifteen minutes. Wasting time, Colonel."

"Do something!" Gregarov screamed, dropping his cigarette, jumping up from his chair.

"You will tell us where the other bombs are," Kisigin demanded.

"A deal. I show you . . . you let me go."

Kisigin hesitated. Carter knew the man was thinking about his reputation. The Russian had picked a bad time to think about pride.

"Come on!" Carter urged. "It's a big place. We've got just enough time."

"For God's sake! Do it, Colonel!" Gregarov bleated.

"All right. Untie him," Kisigin ordered.

"I'm going to my lab," Gregarov said, rising unsteadily, fear blazing from his eyes. He looked more like a frightened animal than ever.

"I'll need all of you," Carter said, a plan forming in his aching head.

"He's right," Kisigin said. "We stick together on this."

"But my lab . . ." Gregarov pleaded.

"You damned coward," Berof said. "You want to make a run for it. I've had it with you. You stay!" he commanded in a voice of steel.

Major Lobanov had untied Carter. The Killmaster stood up and leaned on the chair for a moment, faking dizziness.

"Come!" Kisigin said, grabbing him by the elbow. "We have little time." He looked at his watch. "Less than ten minutes."

"*If* the timers are set at the same time as your watch," Carter commented.

Gregarov whined as Kisigin pulled Carter to the door. Berof had to grab Gregarov by the arm. They made a sad-looking parade as they exited the small room for the cavern.

"Now. Where's the first one?" Kisigin asked.

"The engineering office. Under the cantilevered supports," Carter told them readily enough.

As they started out, Kisigin's hand firm on his elbow, Carter felt for the egg-shaped gas bomb at his crotch, but he was unable to reach it. Walking, the feel of the tape was there. But he couldn't be sure.

At the base of the engineering office, Kisigin let go of his arm. Carter went for the concealed bomb immediately, pulled off the timer, and turned to them. Time was now critical. He couldn't cause a delay. "The dry docks," he said.

They paraded past scores of workers and guards who stared. Kisigin had Carter by the elbow and propelled him along as quickly as he could. Every few seconds he looked at his watch. The color of his face had changed to a pasty white. Berof had Gregarov by the elbow. They followed along, the younger man almost dragging the reluctant older one. The major brought up the rear.

At the dry docks, Carter went unerringly for the bomb and disarmed it. As he stood again, he asked the time.

"Three minutes," Kisigin responded. "Where are the others?" His voice cracked. He wasn't alone in his fear. Gregarov was shaking so badly, he had lost control of his bladder. Berof had cast him aside in disgust.

"One other. The explosives shack. Hurry!" Carter said, jogging under his own power. "I'll need your help. Hurry!"

They approached the wooden shack and the major balked. "I'll stay outside," he said.

"I need you to help me find it," Carter said.

"We all go," Kisigin said, leading the way into the shack.

"Look for a ball of plastic explosive with a timer sticking out of it. I think I put it between two boxes of TNT," he said from the door.

They searched as if fear drove them with a whip. Carter stood back, near the door, his hand closing over Pierre. Beautiful little Pierre. Reliable little Pierre.

Kisigin found the bomb, pulled the timer, and turned to face Carter, his face cruel, his lips curled back reflecting what was to come.

"A deal. Now you let me go. Right?" Carter grinned.

"You fool!" Kisigin shouted, his face red, sweat dripping from his chin. He drew his gun. "Americans! I spit on all Americans! Soft! All too soft!" The gun was coming up. "Good-bye, American," he said with a sneer.

Carter kicked the weapon from his hand, twisted the top off Pierre, took a deep breath, and released the gas in the middle of the room.

He turned and was out the door in a split second. He held it shut for a moment but felt no resistance. "Good-bye, comrades," he said.

He turned from the shack, noted that none of the workers were paying any attention to him, and headed for the sea.

TEN

It seemed to Carter as if he'd been gone for days as he closed the boathouse door and climbed in the old truck Jock Fraser had left for him. All hell would break loose now. The enemy was fully aware of him, the cavern had not been blown, and as far as he knew, Margate, the real prize in this puzzle, was still alive and well somewhere near London.

His mind was torn between the death of the mole, Margate, and the destruction of the cavern. It would be easy if his quarry would show up at the cavern and be blown up with it. But that would depend on luck, or Carter would have to go after him. He knew luck was a sometime thing. He'd have to find Margate's haunts and bring him north.

The old Bedford bumped over the rutted roads in town, sometimes on the left side of the road, where it belonged, and sometimes on the right where Carter normally drove. It was a stake truck, smaller than he was used to, and ancient. Paint was scratched off most of the body. The instrument panel consisted of a gas gauge and a long-dead odometer. The man from AXE found it odd sitting in the right seat with the left empty. Shifting with his left hand was even more strange. He'd driven in Hong Kong and Barbados and other former British colonies who kept to the old system, but he never got used to it.

Out of town, the road was a single lane, the asphalt cracked every few feet. Sheep, wild and shaggy, demanded right of way, so the short trip to the farmhouse was a start-and-stop routine, including waiting for the four-legged locals to cross the road. The whole thing seemed more like a journey than a three-mile drive.

He turned off at the grassed-in lane leading to the farm. The road had been traveled recently. He felt for his Luger and remembered it was hidden in the old house.

As he approached, his lights off, he saw a motor home pulled up at the house. It was a model he'd seen before in Aberdeen and Glasgow. They were mostly rented by American tourists. Carter cursed his bad luck and thought of the cache of weapons he'd left scattered on the floor of the kitchen.

He parked the Bedford quietly, away from the house, and crept up to a lighted window.

Whoever was in the house had his lantern going. It was sitting on the kitchen table. Someone, dressed in black, was sitting with his back to the window. The intruder had put on the other set of black fatigues and the knitted cap.

Carter opened the door slowly. It creaked. The black-garbed figure swung around, the other silenced Beretta pointed at Carter's chest.

Carter swung to the side and swiveled one foot at the enemy's head. He saw it was Cynthia just as she saw him. She lowered the gun casually, clicked on the safety, and holstered it.

He stood looking at her for a second or two. She was outfitted as he had been before his raid.

"What the hell do you think you're doing?" he

barked. "I told you to go back to London and keep out of it."

"Assistant station chiefs don't always take orders from agents," she said, her face straight.

"You know better than to cross me. Do you want it official? You're out. O-U-T. Not part of this." He reached for his cigarettes, his habit crying out for smoke deep in his lungs.

"Come on, Nick. It'll be like old times. I never get to work in the field anymore. Just this once . . . this last time."

"We never use that phrase," he said, drawing deeply on the cigarette. "It could very well be your last time.

"Tell you what," he offered. "You call Hawk while I listen. If he says you're with me, then that's it."

"That's not fair. You know what the old boy will say," she said, taking the cap from her head and tossing it at him. "You come to me, to my bed, any time the mood strikes you, and I ask one little favor . . . just this once."

She saw how he looked at her then. She'd gone too far. It had never been like that. It had always been a mutual thing. She'd always welcomed him with open arms. "I'm sorry," she said. "That was uncalled for. But I really want this last chance."

"No. This one's not for you. Look. When I'm assigned one we can do together, I'll ask for you. I promise. But not this time."

She started to pull off the Kevlar jacket as he came over and put an arm around her. "Do me a favor," he asked. "Ask your friend Malone to fly up here with some canisters of knockout gas. I've got an idea." He proceeded to tell her his plan, to get her in the mood to help, then go back with Malone. He really didn't want her on this one. He just had a feeling about it. She meant too much to him to have her splattered all over the bleak landscape of northern Scotland.

She had eased toward his chest, had started to put an arm around him, when he tensed.

"What's the matter?" she asked.

"Be still. Listen!"

They listened for a few seconds.

"I don't hear anything," she whispered.

"A car. Stay just as you are. Try to look busy." He took the Beretta from her belt and headed for the back door. In the early morning light he saw a car parked down the road.

Carter heard a sound off to the left. The faint smell of propane drifted from the house among the sea smells. Carter's acute sense of smell also picked up the aroma of a pipe, just extinguished. Someone, a man in a business suit, stood behind a tree trunk close to the house.

The man was watching the lighted kitchen window. He was about five feet ten. He looked to be about 190 pounds, although he was wearing a Burberry trench coat against the constant spray from the cliffs, so Carter figured his guess could be off.

Carter was still in black, some of the face makeup still intact. He crept silently behind the figure—the man was totally absorbed with the kitchen window—and struck him once on the side of the neck. He caught the body as it fell and dragged it to the door.

"Open up!" he commanded. And as Cynthia opened the door, he pulled the unconscious man in, his heels dragging over the sill.

Cynthia reached for the man's tweed hat and pulled it from his head.

"It's Terry Wills!" she exclaimed, tossing the hat on the table.

"Who the hell is he?" Carter demanded. "How do you know him?"

"Chief inspector. Scotland Yard. Criminal Investigation Division," she said, sitting on one of the kitchen chairs. "We've bumped into each other on a couple of cases. Had dinner with him once. Not a bad guy, really."

Wills was starting to groan and come around. He opened his eyes and struggled to a sitting position. "Cynthia! Who the bloody hell hit me?"

He followed Cynthia's gaze and saw Carter, dressed in black, his battle dress dirtied, his black makeup smudged. "I knew it!" he exclaimed. "Something big's going on here."

"Terry, what are you doing here?" Cynthia asked.

The CID man grabbed a chair and pulled himself up. He reached for his pipe and jammed it in one side of his mouth. "Vacation, old girl. Heard about this business, the fact that the local chap, Penny, I think, was keeping it under wraps." He lit the pipe and went on in a cloud of his own making. "My spies told me you'd had an overnight visitor and then took off with Malone in his old crate."

"Sometimes it pays not to know too much," Carter warned.

"Don't you look like the innocent one, though," Wills said. "I know much more, Mr. Nick Carter. Figured it out after dear Cynthia and I rubbed shoulders once too often."

"Maybe you know too much for your own good, Terry," Cynthia said. "This one is off limits. Your people have been specifically waved off."

"Vacation, old girl. Nothing official." He grinned. He was a pleasant enough man with a handsome face. And he had many winning ways. At any other time he might be welcome company. But now he was treading on toes.

"You'd be well advised to keep out of this, Wills. If you get in my way, you could get hurt," Carter said, his voice cold.

"Ah, the best of them all . . . the intrepid Killmaster. I'll try to keep out of your line of fire," Wills said as he let loose another cloud of smoke.

"You will excuse us," Carter said to Cynthia as he rose from his chair. He beckoned Wills to follow him to the door. On the way he grabbed the man's hat. When both stood outside, Carter plopped the hat on Wills's head, said good-bye, re-entered the farmhouse, and slammed the door.

"How did he know so much about me?" he asked Cynthia.

"I don't know. He didn't get it from me. But he's a very clever man. Maybe too smart for his own good."

"All right. Forget it for now," Carter said, still breathing heavily, not from exertion, but from anger. "You get out of that rig, call Malone, and get him up here with the gas. Then you're going back to London, old girl," he said, imitating Wills. "And that's final."

"Where are you going?" she asked as they both started to change.

"To the local pub. I want to know if Penny's been acting as predicted and if the old boys are all behaving themselves."

Yuri Gregarov sat in the communications room, a part of the engineering complex. He was being indecisive, as usual.

"You have to call Comrade Margate," a young officer insisted. Captain Josef Persov had taken command on the death of Major Lobanov. He was younger than his predecessor, about thirty, handsome, slightly overweight, which gave his face a babylike quality, and he was extremely ambitious. He followed the party line in everything. It was his path to the top and he never diverged from it.

Persov had found Gregarov sitting against the rock wall of the cavern and had led him to the explosives shack. Together they had discovered the bodies of Kisigin, Berof, and Lobanov. He had ordered the bodies be bagged in black plastic for transport home. Now he was trying to get the new first in command to make the two calls, one to Margate, and one to Moscow. It had not been easy. The man was a fool and a coward. Persov couldn't understand anyone who diverted from the party line. They were all radicals or shirkers . . . nonpersons. This one could contribute so much, but he lacked backbone. He was a jellyfish. If it were his choice, they would get rid of all the weak ones like him, and leave room at the top for men of vision and strength.

Persov finally picked up the telephone, dialed Margate's number, and handed the instrument to Gregarov.

"The Margate residence. Who is this?"

"Tell Mr. Margate this is Yuri Gregarov. It's an emergency."

"He's still asleep. I never wake him when he is sleeping. You'll have to call at a decent time." The voice was that of an imperious English butler.

Persov had been listening in. He snatched the telephone from Gregarov who had sat silent, not knowing what to do.

"This is Captain Persov. Tell Mr. Margate this is an

emergency. If he does not hear about it immediately, he will be very annoyed. Now, get him, quickly!"

It took about three minutes. Margate came on, annoyed.

"This had better be an emergency. Who the hell is this?"

"Captain Persov, sir. Major Lobanov is dead."

"What? Tell me how it happened. And make it slow and clear." The voice had lost its aggressiveness, was cool and concerned.

"The man you wanted interrogated returned as a kind of commando. He planted bombs with timers at several locations within the project. But he was caught by my men. He was questioned by Colonel Kisigin and led them to the bombs—"

"Who the hell is Kisigin?" Margate cut in. "And who are the ones he led to the bombs?"

"The colonel is the one you sent for . . . you know . . . from the Serbsky Institute."

"And . . . ?"

"The others were Colonel Berof, Major Lobanov, and Yuri Gregarov."

"And he disarmed the bombs? Why is Lobanov dead?" Margate demanded impatiently.

"They are all dead. All except Gregarov. He is here with me," Persov explained.

"Then why did he not call me himself?" Margate asked.

"He did . . . I dialed the number for him . . . the butler wouldn't let him talk . . ."

"I understand. But the rest isn't making sense. How did they die? And what's this about Berof being a colonel?"

"The man came back to plant the bombs. My men captured him. He was interrogated. He led them to disarm the bombs, but when he got to the last one, he tossed a gas bomb he had concealed on his body. It killed the three of them in the munitions shack.

"Colonel Berof turned out to be head of the Third Department of the First Chief Directorate, KGB. I heard him tell the major he had decided to come here to evaluate your performance himself. Colonel Kisigin did the same," Persov went on, trying to ingratiate himself with someone higher on the ladder than himself. "Kisigin was head of Serbsky. Wanted to meet you and make his own evaluation of your value to the state."

"Why wasn't Gregarov with them?" Margate asked.

The young man recognized the depth of understanding Margate must have to ask such a penetrating question. How to answer? Especially with Gregarov sitting right here. His remedy . . . his answer was always the same. The party line.

"Comrade Gregarov was highly disturbed by the interrogation and the search for the bombs. It was very dramatic for a scientist. Before they reached the last bomb, he broke down and was left behind."

"And saved his life as a result. Luck of the weak sometimes," Margate mused as Persov waited. "What have you done personally since then?"

"Equipped my ten best men with commando gear and sent them out on separate patrols," the young man said proudly. "I want to know what's going on in our theater of operations. They have been ordered not to show themselves or to harm civilians. If they find the American commando, they are to kill him and bring his body back to me."

"That's a good move. But don't repeat it."

The line was silent for a minute while Margate thought about the situation. "Two things," he finally said. "Call the First Directorate and tell them to replace

Berof. You'd better call Serbsky and let them know
about Kisigin. Tell them we don't need a replacement
for him."

"What about the major?" Persov asked, his heart in
his throat.

"We don't need to replace him. You can carry on.
But you'd better tell the army about his death. The
bodies will have to be flown out."

"I've got all that, sir," Persov said, swelling with
pride and anxious to make the calls.

"I'm interested that you knew about Berof being a
colonel of the KGB and Kisigin a colonel in charge of
Serbsky," Margate said.

"Yes, sir. I was privileged to be at the interrogation."
The young voice was not as confident now. His lips
trembled as he told the story. "I heard the revelation
myself. It was a surprise. I thought you should know,
sir."

"And Major Lobanov? Was he GRU, Persov?"
Margate asked. "Is it army intelligence you will have to
call about him?"

"No, sir," Persov lied. "I know nothing about that."

Dressed in old clothes, a fisherman's sweater and
jeans, Carter opened the door to the pub and was
greeted by the men who sat there almost every day. He'd
changed his mind about seeing them again after his capture in the cavern.

The men sat as before, at three or four tables, talking,
smoking their old pipes. When he came to them, they
pulled the tables into one large square, and Jack Brodie
started to set up newly filled mugs all around.

"Glad to see you all here," Carter said, walking
around the group, greeting each in turn, his arm on their
shoulders, squeezing, his smile broad and friendly.

"Where's Jock?" he asked.

"He'll be along soon. Dipped his sheep this morning. Chemicals. Got himself burned with the stuff. He's to the clinic at Gairloch," one of the old men said.

"We was thinking you wasn't coming back hereabouts," another of the men said, starting in on his next pint, knowing another would replace it now that Carter had arrived.

"I told you I'd be back. What have you all heard while I've been away? Anything new? What about Penny?"

"He's a sly one, that Penny," Jack Brodie said, leaning across the bar. Maggie joined him, the only woman welcome in this male sanctuary. "He says he caught a man on the cliffs," the barman said. "A thief and housebreaker he was. Penny shot him in the chase. They've got the body down to Glasgow in a morgue."

"Did Constable . . . did Old Alf carry a gun?" Carter asked.

"No. And Penny didn't, if the truth be known," Maggie joined in.

"So they have the case closed as far as the outside world knows. They can keep Scotland Yard off their backs," Carter said, thinking about Terry Wills and wondering where he was and what he was doing.

"Nothing else to tell you," one of the men said. "Anything new?" he asked.

"A CID man's nosing around. On his own time. Name's Terry Wills," Carter offered.

"What do you want us to do about him?" Brodie asked.

"Tell him what you told me about Old Alf and the boy. Don't mention my friend Geoff Hood. Don't talk about Sergeant Penny at all. If you do, say it's up to him, his choice, none of your business. Okay?"

A chorus of voices muttered their assent.

Just then Jock Fraser burst into the pub, out of breath. They all looked his way, surprised.

He went to Carter, stood over him, shaking, trying to catch his breath and get it out. Something had frightened him badly.

"A woman. A woman . . . lying by the road . . . blood. Shot. She's been shot!" he finally gasped.

Carter grabbed him by one shoulder and propelled him out of the pub. The others followed, Maggie Brodie bringing up the rear.

"Show me!" Carter said tightly into Fraser's ear. "Where is she?"

Jock Fraser led him halfway to the small house where he lived and to the ditch at the side of the road. In the shadows was a body you could barely see. It was dressed in black, complete with a knitted cap.

Carter turned her over as Fraser had. He knew the bad news before he saw her face.

Cynthia. She had changed back into the fighting garb after he had left, except for the vest. Except for the goddamned vest! The silenced Walther was still clutched in one hand, the barrel still hot. The holes stitched across her chest were dark red. A small stream of blood had crept from her mouth to one cheek and dried. She wasn't cold.

Dead . . . Cynthia had been dead for less than a half hour . . . while he'd been drinking with the boys. He felt an overpowering wave of guilt wash over him.

He began to hear the voices of his friends filter through the grief: ". . . murdering women in our town . . . going home for my gun . . . protect my family."

"Wait!" he shouted them down. "Wait," he said in a lower voice when he had their attention.

"She was a friend of mine. In the same business. I tried to keep her out of it, but she insisted," he told them.

"They can't do this in our town. It's time we went after them," Fraser said, somewhat recovered.

Carter heard a noise over the voices that the others didn't hear. The chopper was going to the farmhouse. He'd have to get back there soon and make his plans with Malone. He stooped and picked up the dead woman, his friend and lover. He slung the deadly-looking weapon over one shoulder and hoisted her over the other.

Before he set off, he turned to the crowd of men and looked at them, his eyes sad. When he spoke, his message was deliberate. No one could misunderstand. "I am a professional at this. She was a professional. This is our work. It is in your town, yes, but it is not your fight.

"Stay out of it. Please. Stay out of it. I don't want to find you in my line of fire, and I don't want to have to rescue you from some fool stunt.

"Worse. I don't want to find you dead. And that could happen. Sure as there's a god in heaven, you could all be as dead as my friend."

Before they could see the pain in his eyes, he started off at a fast trot that would get him to the farmhouse in minutes. The war had heated up for him. He was going to get those bastards if it was his last job. He was going to get them for her.

ELEVEN

As Carter neared the farm, his breath ragged from the long run, he saw the ancient chopper off to one side. Malone was nowhere in sight.

"Stop right there!" a voice commanded from the side of the house.

Carter stopped and turned toward the voice.

Malone emerged from his hiding place, an army issue .45 automatic in his hand. He saw the burden Carter was carrying and came running. "Carter!" he rasped stopping a few paces away. "What happened? Who the hell's that?"

When Carter didn't answer, he approached tentatively, slipping the gun into a hip holster. When he saw who the victim was and the number of wounds, he fell to his knees, his hands going to his face, his grief evident.

Malone was a hard-bitten veteran of the wars who had knocked around more than his share. He was big and raw-boned, redheaded, and lantern-jawed. On first meeting, he looked like he could chew nails, but he was a caring man and soft-hearted, the main reason he was broke most of the time.

Cynthia's death broke him up completely. Carter left him on his knees and carried the body to the chopper. He found a tarpaulin and wrapped her in it like a shroud. He would call Hawk from London to have her picked up.

Malone was still where Carter had left him. He helped the big man to his feet and led him to the house. At the bottom of a duffle he found a bottle of scotch Cynthia had packed. He peeled off the wrapper, wrenched the stopper off, and handed the full bottle to Malone.

The pilot just looked at the bottle at first, then took it in shaking hands and tipped it to his mouth. He took a long pull, the amber liquid trickling from the corners of his mouth. Still stunned, he handed it back.

Carter took a drink, put the bottle on the dusty floor beside him, and turned to the big man, putting a hand on his shoulder. "She was a close friend. How long had you known her?" he asked.

"Four years. We were close once. Jesus! Oh, Jesus! But you know . . . she was way above me. I knew it and lived with it . . . for the last couple of years." He took a soiled handkerchief from a pocket and blew his nose. "What was it she really did?" he asked. "I never poked in, but I'd like to know now."

Carter didn't hesitate. He had plans for this man. Starting out on the right foot was part of their beginning together. "She was the deputy chief of the London office of a secret intelligence agency. I can't give you details, but she was one hell of a smart lady."

"I heard you tell her to get back to London. You were smarter than me. She talked me into dropping her off at Inverness. I knew she was coming back up here. I should have stopped her."

"Can you really see yourself winning that argument?" Carter asked.

"No. You're right. She was one strong-willed woman," he said. He paused for a few seconds, his brow wrinkled in thought. "What the hell's going on up here?" he asked.

Again, Carter didn't hesitate. Malone was going to be a part of it. He had a right to know, within limits. Besides, Cynthia had trusted him implicitly.

"Okay. Briefly. Very high-level stuff. A deep mole in the British government. He's Russian, but he's lived here since he was a kid. He's also a very rich businessman. The ground below the cliffs here is hollow—one huge cavern. Used to be a naval refueling depot. The mole bought all the land around here. The Russians have built a submarine base in the cavern, mini-subs, right under the noses of the British. I'm going to destroy the mole and blow up the cavern."

"He's responsible for Cynthia's death?"

"Yes."

"Where is the bastard? I'm going to kill him," Malone said, his face a gathering storm cloud as he reached for the bottle.

Carter took his wrist in a grip of steel and lowered the bottle to the floor. "We are going to kill him. And it will work better if we're sober," he said, starting a small grin that showed white teeth. It wasn't a happy grin. It was one that spelled trouble for anyone in his way at the moment.

Malone matched the unholy smile and held out his hand. "I'm your man," he said. "What do we do?"

"Fly me to London," Carter said. "I do all the contact work. That's the way it's going to be. You will have an important role in avenging Cynthia, I promise. But it won't be 'hands on.'"

Malone thought about it for a while. "Okay," he said. "Every man to his specialty. I do the flying."

"Good man," Carter said, rising. "I'm going to change and find a hiding place for these weapons.

Check over your crate. I'll be out in ten minutes."

As he peeled off the blood-soaked clothes and changed into the clothes he'd worn from London, Carter lined up in his head the things he'd have to do, in order of priority. As he buckled on the rig for his Luger and strapped the stiletto's sheath to his arm, he knew he'd have to call Hawk first, then go after Margate. He slipped his pants down again and taped a new gas bomb to his inner thigh as he contemplated the menace that was the Squire, Geremy Farnsworth Margate.

He would soon have the bastard. He didn't know where to find him, but that would come. He would find him and it would be the end for the man who was probably aiming for the prime minister's job.

As he walked to the chopper, he thought about restraint. It would take all of his willpower to keep from killing the man on sight. This one time, he wasn't sure he could manage the control that would be required.

Malone wasn't the only one mourning Cynthia. She'd been a very special person in Carter's life. It was hard for him to believe she was gone.

The big man opened his desk with a key attached to his watch chain and opened a drawer. He took out a wooden box, polished and shiny, and extracted a black phone from it. It was an unlisted phone and free from any surveillance. He had it checked by the guards daily.

The man they called the Squire dialed a ten-digit code and then seven other digits. The sequence took him to Russia via East Germany and finally to his contact at the Kremlin. This man was his fourth contact since Sam Margate, his erstwhile father, had been recalled. He had not known the names of any of them. Like him, when the special phone rang, they knew it could only be one person.

"You heard from Persov?" he asked.

"Indirectly."

"I learned one of the dead was Kisigin, head of Serbsky. Another was Berof, head of the Third Department in the First Chief Directorate. I also believe Major Lobanov was GRU."

"Persov is probably GRU as well. These things shouldn't concern you," the contact said. "You should be flattered. They will try to dig, to find out exactly who you are and when you went under. But they will never know. You have supreme control."

"Project Cavern is going sour. It could compromise me. I'm not sure it's worth that."

"It isn't. We have better things for you. The prime minister will soon be on her way. Her successors will have misfortunes. Six years at the most."

"I'm going to give it one more chance. If Project Cavern continues to give me problems, I pull the plug."

"You have our blessing."

"Who initiated this one?" Margate asked. He seldom asked such a question.

"You'd be better off not knowing." A long pause followed the statement. "But I will tell you." Another pause. "The international plan was conceived by the KGB director himself. The premier insisted you not be compromised."

Margate hung up, stunned for the first time by the realization of the enormous power he had attained. He could see it all now. To him, it had always seemed like an important plan. But he now looked at it through the premier's eyes for the first time. The supreme Soviet leader wanted to control the British prime minister's office. It would be the coup that would go down in Soviet history and give the premier immortality.

And Geremy Farnsworth Margate's name would be

whispered with that of the great man.

They landed at Gatwick, on the far side of the field from the tower, near a hangar surrounded by U.S. Army surplus choppers and prop aircraft. Men who looked like carbon copies of Malone walked around in greasy coveralls or worked beneath fuselages, only their feet showing.

"I need to use a phone," Carter told Malone as they walked to the hangar.

"We got a phone." He said it as if it were a major accomplishment. He was part of the fringe element, a man living on the edge, broke one day and flush the next.

Once in the office, with the door closed, Carter dialed the codes that connected him to the AXE communications computer and ultimately to Hawk.

The older man recognized an inflection in his prize agent's voice that spelled bad news. "What happened?" he asked, his voice losing some of its gruffness.

"Cynthia's gone."

"Good Lord! How?"

"She went with me to transport my equipment. I urged her to return to her job, but she hung back and they caught her in the open."

"You're blaming yourself," Hawk said bluntly, his sympathy covered by his curt manner. "She'd been after me for weeks for a field job. It was Cynthia's choice."

"I need to know where Margate is. I'm taking him north when I return."

It was a product of their long and close association that made it unnecessary for Hawk to ask questions. He could anticipate. "He's at his country place south of London for a day or two."

"Where, exactly?"

"Place called Dorking. Junction of A25 and A24 highways. His place is off A25, west of town toward Guilford. Name on the gate out in plain sight. G. F. Margate," Hawk said, as if reciting from a report. "Where are you, precisely?" he asked.

"Gatwick. Far side of the field with the fringe pilots. Got a chopper pilot on the payroll, friend of Cynthia's."

"You know I don't approve of that."

"He's okay. We're going to pay him and cut him loose when he helps me pull this off." It was a tone Carter seldom used with his boss. He could imagine Hawk's mouth twitching around his cigar, but he got no argument.

"About the house. You're in luck," Hawk said. "Dorking is close to you. Take A26, the Brighton road, toward London, and then west along A25. It's about a half-hour drive."

"What's your plan?" Carter asked. "With Cynthia dead, I mean."

"I'll fly over there right away. I want to talk with our top London people. If you need me, I'll be at the Dorchester."

"Thanks. One thing. A crew for Cynthia's body."

"You have her with you?"

"On the chopper at a hangar across the tarmac from the tower. Ask for Jake Malone."

"Take care, Nick."

"Not to worry. Not this time. This one is going to be clean . . . very clean and very swift."

"I know you too well. And I don't feel overly confident. You're letting Cynthia's death affect you. Be careful."

"You're damned right I'm letting it affect me! But you don't have to worry. I'm under control. It's okay.

I'll call you at the Dorchester if I need you."

The battered old van Malone had provided worked its way through traffic at dusk, to the junction of the Guilford road. Carter, dressed as a mechanic, sat at the wheel and concentrated on driving on the right side of the road, right meaning left in this case. He headed into the setting sun, the bright leaves on the trees turning to a dark green, then almost black.

A mile beyond the last house at the outskirts of Dorking, he barely saw the sign. It was almost dark and no moon showed through the overcast.

The house was hidden back in the acreage, surrounded by a high stone fence. Carter drove to the gates. They were steel, twelve feet high, capable of keeping out the most intrepid trespasser.

The Killmaster remembered the house up north. It had been a wall not difficult to climb, but patrolled. Margate also had guard dogs at the northern property. Security could be the same here.

He was going to take no chances. He had all night if necessary. More than that. If it didn't work tonight, he could work at it for as long as Margate remained in the London area. The timing on this job was a luxury for a man in his kind of business.

Carter drove the truck to a grove of trees several hundred yards from the wall. He spilled from the seat and checked his weapons. They were in place. He also carried a tranquilizer gun in case he ran into dogs. He didn't like them. Too unreliable. But it was all he could pick up on short notice.

He scaled the wall near a tree where he would not be in silhouette. The small binoculars he'd shoved in a pocket showed him the house up close. It was all stone, partially covered with the green of ivy. It could contain as many as seven or eight bedrooms, more than forty thousand square feet, plus god-only-knew how many bathrooms and basements.

Guards patrolled the house. He saw no guard dogs, but he dropped to the ground and kept close to the wall all the way around looking for kennels. He saw none.

After using the binoculars, Carter had donned special glasses to detect security beams. He'd eased his way over or under several laser beams in the one circuit he made of the inner wall. He examined the grounds between him and the house carefully and could see other beams crisscrossing the manicured lawns.

He found a weakness. No beams cut across the long driveway to the house from the gates. The surface was crushed stone, impossible to traverse without making some noise. It was the best bet he had. He either took it or made another plan—for another time.

The mechanic's coveralls were an excellent camouflage. He had donned black sneakers and a knitted wool cap. He blended with the night and the profusion of shrubbery.

He was halfway up the drive when a guard turned a corner of the house. Carter ducked behind some shrubs and waited. The man came on, crunching gravel underfoot. He would be gone in a minute.

A dog growled. Carter took a deep breath. He'd miscalculated: they kept the dogs inside and patrolled with them at irregular intervals.

He had little time to think. The dart gun was stuck in the back of his belt under the coveralls. Quickly, he rolled over and reached for the gun as the dog was let loose and came for the bushes in a rush.

Carter ducked the charge and shot a dart into a hairy rump as it passed him by.

The dog returned, jaws agape, his teeth looking twice

their normal size up close. As his mouth closed over Carter's arm, he expected pressure, but it just wasn't there.

Slowly, the animal rolled to one side. He was out of the fight.

The guard hadn't uttered a word; he stood about ten feet away, the barrel of his revolver pointing at Carter's gut.

No man is fool enough to charge a gun, not even a man as skilled as Carter. He waited for the errant moment when the man's eyes turned to the dog, then he flicked his razor-sharp stiletto into his hand. When the man looked back and waved with the gun for Carter to move with him, his gun hand swung in an arc, away from a line of fire.

The knife slipped from Carter's hand as his wrist flipped the sliver of steel. It found its mark in the guard's throat. The man grabbed for his throat as blood flooded his lungs and drowned him.

Carter had not come here to kill, but as often happened, circumstances had moved beyond his control. He had to accept the conditions of the moment.

Margate slept in the master bedroom. He had not been able to sleep at first. Instead, he had watched Beverley as she pulled a brush through her hair a hundred or more times. He used to love the routine. He had been much younger then. She had been slim and desirable. She would come to him, expecting love, her arms a willing enclosure to hold him and her body a ready receptacle that had been a sanctuary.

Time had changed their relationship. A maid had expertly applied a mud pack to her face and she'd sat with the brush in her hand, her mind filled with more decorating nonsense that would cost him a fortune.

With his background of death and deceit, it had occurred to him to rid himself of her as he did with many
of his problems. But it wouldn't work for him. A politician's wife was an asset, especially one who had the
family connections and friends Beverley had. No, he'd
decided, it would be an association that would last the
rest of his life.

She slept beside him in the mammoth, canopied bed
while the works of long-dead masters looked down on
them. Millions of dollars of artwork kept them company every night, a featherheaded socialite and the most
powerful mole in anyone's arsenal of undercover
agents.

The bedroom door opened. A head covered with a
knitted black hat looked around the door and observed
the room for a moment. Carter had come across only
one more guard. The man had been on the lower floor,
busy making himself coffee when Carter took him with
one chop to the back of the neck.

He'd found only two servants. A man and a woman
slept on the third floor. He'd bound and gagged them
loosely. They would be able to free themselves eventually.

Looking from room to room for the Margates, the
number of art treasures had surprised Carter. He'd seen
no alarms inside the house. Apparently Margate was
like many rich men, refusing to have any contraptions
inside the house that could complicate their private
lives.

Now he'd found their bedroom. It was one huge
room that took up the back of the second floor. Two
people slept in the bed. He recognized Margate. A
woman slept beside him. With the mud pack and the

terry turban, she could only be the mistress of the house.

As he watched, Margate's eyes opened. They swiveled to him. Fingers reached for the night table.

Wilhelmina was steady in Carter's hand. "Try that and I shoot wife."

Margate pulled his arm back to the bed. Carter moved swiftly, retrieved a .357 magnum from the night table, and stuffed it into his belt.

"It be more good if you come quiet," Carter said, waving the big man from his bed with a flick of his gun.

The weight of Margate shifting woke his wife. She turned and Carter noted she wore both eyeshades and earplugs to sleep. She slowly pulled the earplugs from her ears and slipped the eyeshades up to her turban.

"What's going on, Geremy? Who is this man?" she asked, her hazel eyes wide with fear.

An idea had occurred to Carter as he'd driven from Gatwick. He would give the prime minister a smoke screen, something to keep the press busy and sympathetic. It would appear that Margate had been taken by Arab terrorists. He would be taken as a hostage and never returned.

Carter swore at the woman in Arabic. "*Halas!*" he said. "Enough!" Then he continued with the accent of an Arab commando speaking very poor English. "The womans will be quiet or we must kill. She must be quiet. It must be!"

Carter shifted Wilhelmina to his left hand and pulled out the small leather case Cynthia had given him up north. It was identical to the one he'd lost climbing the cliffs. A syringe was ready.

"Give arm, Mr. Geremy," Carter said in the same broken English, using the man's first name in the Arab fashion. "If you do not, the woman's head I will bad hurt."

"You'll probably do it anyway," Margate said.

Beverley Margate sat up, petrified, tears running from her eyes as she cried silently.

Suddenly Margate lunged for Carter's head as the Killmaster was about to apply the needle. The Luger described a short arc and clubbed the big man to silence.

Beverley Margate screamed. A long, piercing scream. Carter retrieved the syringe. He pushed it into her arm as the noise from her tortured throat continued to an unresponsive audience.

He gave her only a small dose. Before her eyes started to dull, he spoke in her ear, menacingly: "Tell them we are the Holy Warriors of the Jihad. Tell them Mr. Geremy is only the first."

As her head slumped back onto the pillow, Carter plunged the same needle into Margate's arm and gave the rest of the dose to him.

Now he had to hurry. He picked up the inert body, positioned it over one shoulder, and headed for the door. His thoughts were divided between carrying the big man all the way back to the truck and Cynthia's death. This bastard had killed her. He had probably killed many to get where he was.

It was almost over. Margate would die as prescribed by Hawk, but not today. The Killmaster thought about how he would finally carry out his assignment. He would blow up the project with Margate in it. Poetic justice. The thought sustained him as he carried his heavy burden to the front door and across the grounds.

TWELVE

Beverley Margate slowly came to in the big bed alone. She stayed prone for a few minutes trying to shake the nightmare that persisted no matter how she tried to forget it. In the end, she was forced to remember the terrorist sticking her with a needle. She found the spot, a drop of dried blood, and she had to face a terrifying fact.

Geremy had been kidnapped.

Years of pampering by her parents and indulgence by her husband had given her the reputation of being first a spoiled brat and later a useless matron. Nothing could be further from the truth. She loved the life she led. She had deliberately created the image people had of her. What few people realized was her unqualified value to her husband as a political campaigner. She knew how to exploit every situation, sometimes using the image of a dedicated wife and mother as a screen. She knew all the angles, the value of political position and how to use it.

So, after making a tour of the house and finding the dead guard, she headed for the nearest phone. She was sure Geremy had been taken. The memories were too real for it to have been a bad dream. God, it had been all too real. The first thing she did was to call the prime minister. When you wanted results, you went to the top.

"Don't tell me she's at a meeting," she told the P.M.'s secretary. "This is Beverley Margate. Tell her it is the most critical crisis to hit her government since she took office. *Do it now!*"

The prime minister was on the phone in seconds. It was obvious to Beverley that the woman had been within earshot all the time.

"What is it, Beverley?" the iron lady asked without preliminaries.

"Geremy has been taken by Arab terrorists. They killed one of my guards and drugged me."

"Good God! How long ago?"

"I'm not sure. It must have been at least six hours ago."

"Have you called anyone else?"

"No."

"Did they leave a message with you?"

A haunting memory suddenly assailed her. *Tell them we are the Holy Warriors of the Jihad. Tell them Mr. Geremy is only the first.* The words came back as clearly as she'd heard them. She repeated them to the prime minister. "He kept using Geremy's first name," she told her powerful friend. "He said 'Mr. Geremy' all the time. I've traveled in the Middle East enough to know some Arab customs. He was an Arab, all right."

"What did they look like?"

"I only saw one. He wore dark clothes and—" Her resolve melted then and she broke down. "Oh dear, what are we to do?" she sobbed.

"They'll want something. We just have to wait until we hear from them. I'll call the home secretary immediately."

"I'm coming up to London," Beverley said, getting hold of her emotions. "I'll stay at the flat until we hear from them."

"Let my secretary know when you get in. Get a friend

to stay with you, Beverley. I'll ring off now and get something started.''

When she sat alone on the bed again, Beverley thought about her marriage. A lot of it had been hollow—meaningless. But Geremy was a powerful man, politically and in the business world. It was necessary for him to be away from her, natural for him to be preoccupied with his interests. She had accepted this and had learned to live with it. After all, her life had not been too unlike her mother's or her friends'.

She shuddered as she contemplated his not coming back. Life had not been hollow at all when she considered what it would be if he didn't come back. He *had* to come back.

Carter sat in the chopper, strapped against the rolls and jerks of the bumpy air at low altitude, thinking about the events of the last two days. Malone flew the machine and didn't say a word. Carter knew why: the pilot was still too shaken by Cynthia's death. Hawk's people had picked up her body just after he returned with Margate. Carter remembered the look on Malone's face as he watched them cart her away. He felt the same but steeled himself against showing a reaction, at least until this was over. They had planned to go away together for a few days. Perhaps it would really hit him then.

He looked over his shoulder at the prostrate Margate. The big man had tried to sit up, but his bonds had constrained him, leaving him half sitting and half lying. He had to be cramped and uncomfortable. Hate poured from the blue eyes. If he ever got loose, he would be dangerous, much more dangerous than the image he had cultivated.

Carter had not thought ahead, had not figured things down to the last detail. In his experience, too many plans had gone wrong for him to plan everything. He knew he had to somehow render the whole staff at the cavern unconscious, then get them out before he blew it. He had been ordered to kill only one man, not perform a massacre. And he had to make sure Margate was in the cavern when it blew. Another thread to tie in.

He was still thinking, sorting possibilities, when the aircraft crossed over into Scotland and the Highlands loomed ahead.

Douglas Weatherby had been a friend of the prime minister since their early days in the stumpings. They had met at rallies and stood up for each other, extolling each other's merits. They had even remained friends during and after the leadership race when the strong-willed woman prime minister captured the imagination of the whole world.

The Honorable Douglas Weatherby could have been named to any of several top positions in her government. But the P.M. had wanted someone she could trust in charge of her police and intelligence services—someone she could trust with her life. So Weatherby was home secretary, privy to more secrets of hers than she of his.

They sat is a small study at 10 Downing Street. It was the prime minister's favorite room when she was in town. It had been decorated for a man, probably Wilson. The decorator used wood paneling and stone almost exclusively, but the current occupant had added a few feminine touches of her own, hanging plants and small tapestries. No great masters hung here. The prime minister was known for her frugality. The room was comfortable and functional. And it had the best-drawing fireplace in Westminster. It was constantly lit during the frequent chills of London.

"To quote the Americans, 'you're caught between a rock and a hard place,' " the jovial Weatherby said.

"I don't think so," the prime minister responded. "The president assured me he had put their best man on it. Geremy will disappear along with the project he's working on."

"I do wish you'd have let me handle it," he said.

"I know, Doug. Normally I would have. But Geremy's place in my government was just too strong. The pundits had me moving you up and him replacing you." She drank from a delicately formed china teacup before going on. "No. It had to be outside your office."

"They sent one man. Just one man. I can't believe it."

"I can. I've seen his work before." She smiled and almost laughed as she went on. "Taking Margate and making it look like a terrorist raid was a stroke of genius."

"I've got to admit, I like it. Gives you the perfect out."

"I wonder if the Arabs will take credit. It would make it so much easier if they do," she said softly, as if to herself.

"The home secretary was with the prime minister this morning," the man from MI5 said.

"And she had a call from Mrs. Margate this morning," the man from MI6 responded.

They were in the office of a chief superintendent of Scotland Yard. It was a small office at the New Scotland Yard Building, mostly glass, the furniture at least twenty years old.

It was unusual for the three services to work together,

but they had all seen scraps of evidence that something big was going on. Whatever it was, one of them should have been involved. But none was.

"My chief has received calls from the head of a low-profile service in Washington," the man from MI5 said.

"David Hawk," the chief superintendent said.

"Who?" MI6 asked.

"I should have thought you'd know the name," Scotland Yard said. "David Hawk," he repeated. "Donovan and the OSS. Helped him form the CIA later. My people tell me his outfit, whatever it is, takes on covert work the president doesn't want the CIA to handle."

"I should think that would be all of it, the way they've messed things up," MI6 said, an amused smile on his face.

"It's related to the Scottish thing, isn't it?" MI5 asked. "The one we warned that fellow off? Name was James Long. Staying at the Royal Court."

"Yesterday's news, old chap," MI6 said. "He's checked out and disappeared. I suspect he's one of this fellow David Hawk's people."

"While you were all asleep at the switch, one of my people went on holiday and is staying at Poolewe." Scotland Yard smiled wickedly. He picked up his pipe, lit it with a kitchen match, and blew smoke to the ceiling.

"That's a weak dodge," MI6 complained. "We were all told to keep clear."

The MI5 man was about to shout out a protest, but he shrugged and spoke in a normal voice. "Now that you've bent the rules, tell us what he's found," he urged.

"A woman by the name of Cynthia Talbot was up

there. Introduced my man to a chap called Nick Carter," he said.

"Carter," the MI6 man said, rubbing his chin. "I've heard of him. Some kind of superagent. Who's this woman Talbot?"

"Works for Amalgamated Press and Wire Services in .London. A Washington-based outfit," Scotland Yard said.

"It doesn't add up," MI6 said. "Why would she know a foreign agent? What the hell's she doing in Poolewe?"

"The whole thing stinks. Especially when you add the fact that I have a report she was killed in Scotland and her body brought back south," MI5 said. "Came across my desk this morning."

"I'll be damned!" Scotland Yard said. "Today, you say? Why the hell didn't I have a copy?"

"Have you heard from your man lately?" MI6 asked.

"No." Scotland Yard was pensive. "Long overdue as well."

"I tried to open up the old man this morning," MI5 said. "Attitude worse than ever. He told me to lay off at risk of my job. This meeting is as far as I'm going to go. You could have your ass in a sling for sending a man up there."

"Too late now," Scotland Yard said. "Too late."

"The whole thing stinks," MI6 said. "Sounds very big, this one. We should be on it. Looks like the brass asked the Americans for help, if you ask me."

"Must be political," MI5 said. "Trouble is, they're blowing it. I've got a feeling they're blowing it."

Coming in over Poolewe, Malone circled out to sea and came at the farm from the cliffside. He gently set the old chopper down facing toward the house and close to the old Bedford.

Carter stepped down first and pulled Margate by the heels to the edge of the door. He tried to hide his emotions as much as possible on a job, but this man could be the most important mole in the history of intelligence work. He had probably ordered up scores of killings in his time. He had certainly been responsible for Cynthia's death.

Carter knew he'd have to watch Malone, too. As much as Carter needed the flyer right now, the man was almost irrational with grief. He'd probably kill Margate if left alone with him.

Carter hoisted Margate over one shoulder, carried him to the farmhouse, and when Malone opened the door, dumped him in a corner of the dust-covered living room.

"What now?" Malone asked.

"Outside," Carter said, inclining his head.

He led the way outside, pulled his cigarettes from his pocket, and flamed one with his lighter. The breeze from the sea was as strong as ever. He had to talk loudly, over the sound, as he led Malone away from the house.

"Cynthia asked you to bring some pressure tanks and fittings on your last trip."

"Yeah. They're in a back room." Malone reached into his filthy coveralls and pulled out a joint. He lit it, dragged the smoke deep into his lungs, then held his head back, letting the drug course through his body, giving him new life.

"You got any more of those?" Carter asked.

"No. Sorry."

"Don't be sorry. Just cool it when that one is done. Okay?"

"Shit! You some kind of saint or something?"

"It's not just Cynthia, Jake. The guy back there is probably the most important agent the Soviets have ever infiltrated anywhere. The cavern under our feet is a threat to Western security. It has got to go." He took a deep drag. The smoke disappeared in the wind that tugged at his hair. "You can smoke or drink whatever the hell you like once this is over, but let's get these bastards now and screw around later, okay?"

"Got you," Malone said, pulling in the last of the smoke. His eyes closed slightly as the high relaxed him. "So tell me what to do."

"Wait!" Carter said, pulling him down, holding a hand over his mouth.

Someone was running to the farm as fast as he could. Carter had heard a twig break and a shoe scuffling on gravel. Now the sound was clear. He could even hear the intruder's ragged breath.

Carter pulled his Luger and waited. The figure looked familiar. It was as wide as it was tall. "Jock," Carter whispered. "What the hell brought him here?"

As the short Scotsman approached, the moon shining on his sweat-soaked face, he looked like a cooked lobster, red and steaming.

When he saw Carter he fell to his knees, his head almost between his thighs. He was desperately gulping air, his lungs seeking more oxygen, his mouth working, trying to form words.

"They got . . . worked up . . . after you left. I talked . . . to them and Jack Brodie tried." He sat back on his heels looking up at them, his chest not heaving as fast as it had. "It was okay yesterday. They settled down. But . . . they started up again today. Went for their shotguns."

"What the hell's he talking about?" Malone asked.

"The old boys of the town," Carter said. "Christ. I should have known."

"What does he mean, 'for their shotguns'?" Malone quoted.

"Cynthia's death was the last straw," Carter said. "They let me hold them off when it was just the boy and Old Alf. They were worried but never saw the bodies. Then when they saw a woman with multiple wounds . . . you know what that's like for the first time. And a woman . . ."

Malone turned to ask another question, but Carter had disappeared into the house. He returned almost immediately carrying the Walther machine pistol and a couple of extra clips.

"I'm going to the main gate. That's where they would have headed," he said. He turned to Jock Fraser who had almost regained his breath. "The man behind all this is now a prisoner in the farmhouse. I charge you with his safety," he said, directing his comments to Fraser.

He turned to Malone. "I've got to put you on your honor. I don't have time for games. Leave Margate alone."

"You're going to kill him anyway, aren't you?" Malone asked.

"That's not your concern," Carter said, his eyes cold, conveying a message of their own. "I'm under orders. He may be useful. Do not, I repeat *do not* harm the man."

Malone looked morose . . . uncertain. Fraser had recovered, but he looked different . . . like a man ridden with guilt.

"I don't have time to argue," Carter shouted over his shoulder as he started the old truck and turned it around, spraying gravel.

THIRTEEN

Yuri Gregarov sat at his desk in the engineering section with the door closed. The world had become too complicated for him. From his peasant beginnings as the son of a poor farmer he had become a brilliant student destined for the National Academy. He had made it and had headed up several projects through the years that had enhanced his stature. He had privilege, his own apartment, a dutiful wife, and two sons who had chosen military careers.

But through it all he had been small in stature and courage. The laboratory was his life, the safety of tiled walls, doors with coded locks, and guards patrolling constantly. It had been his security blanket and he felt naked without it.

Project Cavern was not his kind of work. Not what he would have chosen. To be thousands of miles from home, subject to attacks from unknown sources, was not for him. The thought of it brought him awake at night in a cold sweat.

He couldn't believe he had been so close to death a few days ago. Kisigin and Lobanov had seemed so invulnerable, and now they were dead. He had seen one of the enemy, a man in black who seemed beaten at one time and who had turned the tables on them all. What would he do if he were in the power of such a man? He had no courage to resist force. He hated to think about it.

The door in front of him opened and Persov entered uninvited.

"You will not enter without invitation, Captain," he said, his ferretlike face screwed up in a scowl. "What do you want?"

"I've been talking to Grinski at Margate's estate south of London," Persov said, his face ashen with fear. Gregarov had never seen him like this. "He's a guard there," Persov went on. "The man who killed Major Lobanov and the others has taken Margate."

"Taken him? Taken him where?"

"Don't be a fool. He's taken him prisoner. It's over for him," Persov said.

"Tell me what this man Grinski saw. You questioned him, I hope," Gregarov's high-pitched voice wailed.

"The man in black killed the outside guard and overpowered Grinski. He drugged Margate's wife and took Margate with him." He reached for his cigarettes and lit one, his hand shaking. He sat opposite Gregarov in clouds of smoke and shook his head.

"I talked to Margate such a short time ago," the young captain said. "He gave me instructions."

"What instructions?" Gregarov asked.

"To call Moscow, report the deaths here, and to ask for replacements."

"Good God! I never thought of that. Do we really need another Kisigin here?"

"No. He told me not to ask for a replacement for him," Persov said, pulling on his cigarette like a man possessed. The length of ash lengthened magically.

"Good. His kind made my skin crawl."

"We need his kind, comrade. Everyone has a place in the workings of the state."

"Of the KGB you mean," the small man said.

"Dangerous talk, Gregarov. Don't make me report you as a subversive."

"I won't have you talking to me this way! This insubordination will be reported," Gregarov said in his irritating whine. "You will be out of here. Who did Comrade Margate say will be replacing Major Lobanov?"

"No one. Comrade Margate told me to carry on for now."

Gregarov sighed. He looked at the military man, not hiding his disappointment. He had never liked this young idealist. His kind had no place in the world of Yuri Gregarov. "What else did you learn?" he asked.

"The man in black spoke in Arabic. He told Margate's wife he was from an Arab organization, a terrorist organization."

"Who'd believe that?" Gregarov asked.

"Apparently Mrs. Margate does. She's never been a part of this." Persov waved an arm. "She called the prime minister."

"She *what*?"

"Called Ten Downing Street," Persov said, smiling wanly, lighting a second cigarette from the first. "That's just what a woman like her would do. She sees the head of the party—their party—at dinners and rallies. Naturally she would call her."

This was out of Gregarov's league. "Do you think the prime minister believed her?" he asked.

"I don't know. The call would be genuine. It depends on what other information the prime minister has."

"And what does that mean? What else could she know?" Gregarov asked, suddenly very frightened.

"I don't know. But consider this," Persov said. "Margate has been here for forty years, underground.

He's sure to have made some mistakes. This project could be blown.''

"My God! Do you think so?" Gregarov said, his voice a squeak.

"I don't really know. I just look at facts. We have killed three people that I know of—maybe four. We've left loose ends. It all leads back to this cavern or Margate's house across the bay. We could have been seen. We don't know who the man in black is. We know he's no Arab. And he's got Margate," Persov recited, ticking off the points on the finger of one hand.

"But who is he?"

"I don't know," Persov said.

Gregarov wished he was anywhere but in the cavern that he'd begun to think of as his grave. He never wanted to face the man in black again. Somehow he knew they would meet again and he would have no power to resist the man. He was a scientist, not a warrior.

He desperately wished to be back home in Moscow.

As he swung the old Bedford along the rutted road toward the entrance to the cavern, Carter could hear the boom of shotguns and the staccato of Kalashnikovs in the distance.

Fifty yards from the action, he pulled the truck behind a stand of gnarled beech trees and vaulted from it to the ground. Within seconds he was moving fast, from tree to tree, in a crouch.

Directly behind the firefight, he stopped to take in the action. The men from the pub, at least a dozen, were behind trees, ducking out for a shot, exposing themselves to the wicked fire of automatic rifles that poured out steel-jacketed slugs at more than seven hundred rounds a minute.

Jack Brodie was out in front, dragging a wounded sheep man from the fence. While Carter watched, too far away to help, two guards ran from their positions, clubbed Brodie to the ground, and dragged both Scotsmen into the cavern entrance.

Carter whipped the Walther to a firing position and clicked off the safety. He couldn't take a shot. The guards were screened by their prisoners.

"Start to retreat!" he yelled over the firing. "I'll give you covering fire." He assumed a prone firing position, set the firing sequence to three shot, and started to pick off the guards. He had taken down two men when he raised his head to find the sheep men still blasting away.

"Get the hell back to the pub! You can't do anything for them now!" he yelled over the firing.

When they had finally given up, he heard two ancient trucks start up, one backfire, then their rumble gradually fade.

He stopped firing, saw the heads of wary guards edge around abutments.

"I have Margate," he called out. "I'll be back in an hour to exchange him for your two prisoners." He repeated the offer in Russian.

He waited for a few minutes. He got no answer.

"I'm waiting for your answer," he yelled. "I don't want Margate alive. If I don't hear from you—"

"—we are seeking authority. Wait!" one of the guards shouted back.

Finally, a full five minutes later, the same man yelled again: "Bring him in one hour. We will exchange."

Carter raced for the truck. One hour would make it tight, but the last act was in motion and it would have to be played out before all the action attracted other players—unwelcome players.

He drove like a madman to the pub and raced

through the door. They were all there, sitting morosely. Maggie Brodie, tears rolling down her face, was bandaging a wounded arm.

"You fools!" Carter started. "I've got their leader. It would have been all over. But now I have to exchange him for prisoners. Dammit! I told you to stay put!"

"How do you expect us to stay put when they kill at our doorstep? Tell me that," one of the men said.

Carter cooled a little, knowing he would have reacted the same way.

Maggie had finished the bandage and was behind the bar. Out of habit, she was filling pint mugs with frothing beer for her boys.

Carter moved up beside her. "I've made a deal with them. Our two for their head man. Jack will be all right. I promise."

Maggie turned from the spigot and clung to him. "Get my Jack back, mister. Just get him back," she cried.

On the way back to the farm, Carter thought about the turn of events. His trip to London had just been negated. At least partly. They would get Margate back, but the mole's days in England were numbered. Carter would blow the cavern, that he was sure of. But now the cavern and the project it served was compromised and the Russians must know it.

No matter. He had his orders. Margate had to go. Even if the man was finished here, he knew too much to let him be returned to the Soviet Union.

At the farmhouse, he slid the truck to a halt in the dust of the road and sprinted for the door. He'd already used half of the hour. At the door he stopped. Something was desperately wrong. The sharp, sheared-metal smell of blood was everywhere.

Carter pulled his Luger and kicked the door open.

The smell of death assaulted him as he stepped into the room.

Jock Fraser was lying in a pool of blood. He was half the size he'd been in life, was spread out on the floor, a slash of red across his gut, his hands holding his intestines in a death grip.

Margate lay near him, silent and still.

Carter rolled Margate over. The blue eyes looked at him from a deep well of pain. He had been shot in one shoulder. Blood had congealed on his coat and on the floor. A lot of blood.

Malone was finished. His pulse was thready, very weak. He had been gut-shot twice. The gun lay under him, a bloody kitchen knife beside it.

Carter had no time for analysis. His own people had to have been playing games and it backfired. You don't play games with a jungle cat without getting hurt.

"How bad is it?" Carter asked Margate. "Can you walk?"

"Depends."

"On what?" Carter asked.

"On the reason. If I'm still a prisoner, bring the doctor to me. To hell with walking."

Carter clenched his jaw. This was a worthy adversary. Too bad he'd have to let him go. "You've just won a round you didn't know you were playing," he said. "Two of my men in exchange for your worthless hide. The deal's been made."

"Then I can manage to walk a few feet," the big man said, his face creasing in a small smile, as much as he could manage with the pain.

Carter helped him to his feet and to the door. He managed to get him in the truck and under way. He'd have to be more wary than ever now. They'd try to get Margate back to Russia as fast as possible.

Carter decided he'd have to move up his schedule.

As the old truck slid to a stop outside the pub, all the men piled out to cheer and lend a hand. Jack Brodie was unharmed and opened his arms for a weeping Maggie who flew into them. The others carried the wounded man into the pub. He'd live. A round had gone cleanly through an inner thigh, missing the main arteries. Once inside, he accepted a brandy and downed it in one gulp as they tore away his wool work pants.

Without asking permission, Carter headed for the kitchen and the phone. He asked for the Dorchester in London. Hawk was there and on the line in seconds. They made no pretense of secrecy. They had no time.

"What do you mean you've lost him?" Hawk snapped.

"Couldn't be helped." Carter ignored the rebuke. "I'll get him later. Right now I need your help."

"What do you need?"

"I'm going to blow the cavern tonight. I've got a plan in mind. If it works, the Russian personnel will start streaming out the entrance at the top of the cliffs."

"I'll have a detail watching for them."

"I'm going to trap Margate inside the cavern. Right now he'll be at his house on the other side of the bay. If I get the cavern but fail to get Margate, I want a backup detail to take the house.

"I'll do the best I can. I saw twenty subs in the cavern. Each can fire five missiles. God only knows how many they carry. No guarantees, but I'll try to use plastic explosives and whatever else I can find."

Carter was eager to get on with it. He waited for a few seconds for a reply, then hung up the phone.

Hawk knew him as well as any man alive. They thought a lot alike. The older man knew he would do his best, but the job had to be done—one way or the other.

Gregarov had no heart for the kind of work they'd ordered him to do lately. After Persov left, he sat for a few minutes as various scenarios played through his head like scenes in action/adventure novels. He would overcome the man in black and be a hero of the Soviet Union. The man in black would capture him and make him contribute to the scientific knowledge of the West. Margate would recover enough to take the reins again and make the whole scheme work. Being an idealist, the latter solution was the one his shattered psyche chose.

He was about to go down to the seaway entrance and work on one of the subs that had just come in, when the telephone rang.

"Yes. Gregarov."

"General Protopopoff. We heard Comrade Margate has been captured. What is going on there, comrade?"

"General. Yes, he was captured, but I have made an exchange for him."

"An exchange? Who the hell did you have to exchange?"

Gregarov knew this wasn't going to go well. Protopopoff had conceived Project Cavern. He wasn't going to like the whole story. "We had two locals who had attacked the entrance. I got Margate back in exchange for them."

"Two locals? You must be compromised. It's a miracle the army isn't at your door right now," the general said. "We have some replacements in the air now. When they arrive, get everyone out, including Margate. Do you hear me, Gregarov?"

"I hear you, General. I'll do it. I'll tell Margate you called."

When he put down the phone, Gregarov was a different man than the one who had picked it up. Something had snapped under the stress of the last few days. All he could think of was the work he wanted to do on the newly arrived sub. The general's call was forgotten.

He called his favorite assistant and started for the seaway entrance.

FOURTEEN

Sir Aubrey Wilbertson, the chief of internal security, MI5, picked up the cup of tea his secretary filled regularly on the hour, and drained it. He sat behind his desk, a grin on his face, anticipating a morning call from Hawk. He was a small man, shorter than Hawk, thinner and older, but as experienced.

Wilbertson had put a special assistant on Hawk's tail the moment he'd found out that the prime minister had called the Americans for help. The last time the young man had called, he'd reported Hawk had taken a night flight to London and checked into the Dorchester. The head man at AXE would be calling soon. It was a routine they had followed for years.

Wilbertson knew there was no way the head of a covert American agency could handle the current emergency alone. It was something that politicians never seemed to learn. Hawk could comply with their orders, but he would never be totally in the cold. He would need cleanup squads, perhaps some military backup. He had to get them locally.

Did his own prime minister think she could call in the Americans and her own people not know what was going down on their own turf? Did she and the president think Hawk would not call him, or he call Hawk under the same circumstances? The politicians came and went as the fickle moods of the public dictated, but people like Hawk and himself went on forever, or until old soldiers faded away.

The buzzer beside his phone sounded. His secretary had Hawk on the line. Good. He was about to enjoy this.

"David," he said. "Everything satisfactory at the Dorchester?"

"As always," Hawk chuckled, not giving his friend the satisfaction.

"What brings you here?" Wilbertson asked.

"Let's not play games, Aubrey. I told you about the initial play. I need you in for the final curtain."

"I know most of it. Give me the rest," Wilbertson said.

"My man is ready for the finale. Your mole is Geremy Farnsworth Margate."

"Good Lord! That I didn't know."

"Margate has bought up most of the land along the sea from Gairloch to Achiltibuie on the northeast Scottish coast, about sixty air miles northwest of Inverness," Hawk said. The words were staggered as he chewed the end off a cigar and lit it. Wilbertson recognized the interrupted speech. He was familiar with the gesture. He had seen Hawk face to face many times and could imagine again the foul smell of Hawk's brand of cigar.

"The Russians have cleared out all the oil storage tanks used at the former refueling station," Hawk continued. "They've built a service base for a fleet of minisubmarines operating in the North Sea."

"I've had some scraps of intelligence on it. I had a man in mind to take a look."

"They made a mistake," Hawk said, "It's too obvious. Curious locals got in the way. Four people dead so far. Two of them mine."

"Sorry, old chap. I know only too well how that hurts," Wilbertson said. "How close is your man to closing it out?"

"Tonight. I need you to pull some people together for support."

"Name it. How's your man going to play it?"

Hawk hesitated, taking a deep drag on the cigar. Wilbertson thought he knew what was coming. He'd have done the same.

"I'm going to fly to Inverness and hire a car. Unless you can meet me there and we go in together," the American said.

"I'll be at the airport in three hours," Wilbertson said. "But I'd like to know now what to expect. How many people do you need?"

"Right now we need a platoon of marines at the mouth of a cavern they use for the sub pens. Tell them to get directions at the pub in Poolewe," Hawk said.

"From civilians?" Wilbertson asked incredulously.

"They're already involved."

"Dammit to hell!" Wilbertson swore, alarmed. "How the bloody hell do we keep this quiet with all the locals in the act?"

"It'll never be kept quiet. This one is more important than Philby," Hawk said, letting the thought sink in. "He was being groomed as the next home secretary. I'm sure the Russians saw him as a future prime minister."

"Is that all you need from us?" Wilbertson asked. He was stunned but tried not to let it show.

"No. Margate has a huge house on the coast west of Achiltibuie. My man hopes to lure him out and down into the cavern before he blows it," Hawk said. "I need another platoon of marines to hang back and watch Margate drive to the cavern. If he doesn't go, we will signal you and you take Margate into custody."

"Why not let us take him anyhow?"

"The P.M. doesn't want Margate around to embarrass her. She doesn't want him back in the USSR spilling his guts, either," Hawk said without emotion.

"All right. We play it your way. I'll get on it right away."

"See you at Inverness, Aubrey," Hawk said, his spirits lightening as the end seemed to be nearing.

"My club here afterward, what? Long time since I've had a chance to entertain visiting VIPs."

"Can it, Aubrey. I'll settle for bangers and mash in Soho. Let's get this over with before we talk of victory. My best man is out there. I want him back, then I'll celebrate."

It seemed to Carter as if he'd been doing this all his life as he stepped from Jock Fraser's old boat and tied it up. He was in full scuba gear, all in black except for the tank. He thought fleetingly about Fraser as he sneaked along the rock to the sea entrance to the cavern. The Scot and Malone just wouldn't listen. They'd tried to take care of Margate themselves and had underestimated the man. Now his job would be a hell of a lot tougher and he'd lost two good men. He'd also lost his prize hostage.

He looked at his Rolex. Not much time. He knew that Margate would figure it out sooner or later and head back to the Soviet Union. Carter had to be quicker. The plan had to coordinate perfectly if it was to work.

Two guards patrolled again. No time for niceties this time. Soldiers sometimes had to pay the price. He went straight in blasting, his silenced Walther pouring out slugs. In a welter of flesh, spewed blood, and chipped bone, the men went flying from their ledge into the ocean.

Carter slipped in a fresh clip of thirty rounds and flipped the empty casing after the bodies. He crept up to the opening. No one was on duty immediately inside the cavern.

He crept in further, holding the Walther at the ready, expecting anything.

No one came. He heard no sound of the enemy moving about. The whole cavern was as quiet as a deserted tomb.

A head popped up from the conning tower of the nearest sub and disappeared again. Carter slipped out of sight, circling around, and came up on the sub from the rear.

He hopped aboard. The sub was big enough not to move or wallow as he stepped onto her and walked silently to the tower.

Someone was down there. The head he'd seen had been bare, not covered with a military cap. Carter moved on rubber-soled shoes to the conning tower. He scrambled down the air lock to the control deck like an agile monkey.

Two men were caught unawares. With their white lab coats, he figured they were technicians or scientists. They stared at him, their action frozen as they stared with fear-filled eyes.

"I remember you," Carter said to the smaller of the two, a man with buck teeth and sharp features. "You're Gregarov," Carter said, satisfied with himself. "You have authority here. That means you know a lot about these machines."

"What does that mean?" Gregarov almost quaked as he spoke. He'd had nightmares about this moment, about this black-garbed man. Nightmares he never expected to exit alive.

"It means you will restore this sub to take us out of

here. And it means you will set a timer on one of the other subs to blow a missile and destroy the cavern.''

"No! We can't do that," Gregarov sputtered.

"They will get you for this. Our people will crush you." The other scientist spoke for the first time.

"Who is this, Gregarov?" Carter asked.

"Vilitchin, my assistant. He's harmless. You will not harm him. Please?''

Carter could see the look of the fanatic in the younger man. His kind had been fed the party line at special camps. Like the Arab terrorists, he would fight and die rather than be compromised. To die for the state was an act of honor. He could be a dangerous young man.

Carter held them at gunpoint until he found some wire in the maintenance locker. He tied them hand and foot, placed gags in their mouths, and left them. They were his ticket out of there and his means of destruction.

It took Carter fifteen minutes to reach the top again. He was getting good at it. He found the bunkerlike entrance closed and guarded by two men in uniform. The ducts that carried fresh air to the cavern were located on either side of the entrance.

First things first, Carter thought. He raced back to the farmhouse, returned with the two tanks of gas Malone had brought at Cynthia's instruction, and laid them down beside one of the ducts.

He rested a moment to get his breath. Despite his excellent physical condition, the trip up the cliff and the return journey to the farm had taken its toll. He looked at his watch as his ragged breathing smoothed out. Where did the time go? Hawk would have the military alerted by now. He hoped they would keep out of sight as instructed. Too many times he'd seen overeager amateurs or scared soldiers blast away too soon and screw up a plan.

He left the canister and crept to the sentries. If he'd had more time, or if the situation wasn't so grave, he'd have knocked them out and tied them up. But he had no such choice. He flicked his stiletto into his right hand and stalked each man silently, slitting their throats, stepping clear of the rush of blood, and dragging them back out of sight.

Each canister had a long tube at the throat of its valve. Carter bound the canisters to the ducts and flipped the tubes five feet down, almost to the level of the fans. He opened the valves and waited until the fans sucked the gas into the bowels of the cavern.

Again he checked his watch. It was ten minutes after eleven at night. The gas would keep all the personnel of the cavern unconscious for two hours, give or take a few minutes. Now that he'd set the plan in motion, it was a race against time.

The entrance doors at the top were made of steel, heavy and almost unmanageable for one man. Carter struggled with them, opened them enough to squeeze through, and closed them again.

Guards and technicians were scattered everywhere, unconscious on the rock floor at entry level. Carter ignored them. With his scuba mouthpiece in place, he moved as quickly as possible to the lowest level and the submarine. He used an air lock to get into the sub. The scientists were as he'd left them. Gregarov looked different. Something had given him the confidence to face the enemy.

Desperate for time, Carter issued his orders: "You two are going to make this sub ready for sea. We are going to activate one missile on board to explode on a timer, and another on a second sub that will be left in the cavern. It will be fitted with a radio control.''

"Where are you going to explode this one?'' Vilitchin asked.

"At the base of the cliff below Margate's house.''

"You can't,'' Vilitchin said haughtily. "They'll get to you first.''

"Forget it. Everyone in the cavern is out cold. No opposition there.''

"Comrade Margate has new personnel from home,'' Vilitchin announced.

"At the house?'' Carter asked.

Vilitchin began to wonder if he'd revealed something that he shouldn't have. His mouth became a tightly closed thin line.

"I've been thinking,'' Gregarov said. "You aren't going to make this work. The nuclear devices on the subs would be too powerful. And they would contaminate everything for miles around.'' He sat on his haunches, rubbing his freed wrists, grinning triumphantly.

Carter thought about the Russian's comments. The man was right. He tied them up again and left them cursing as he exited by the air lock.

He checked the time again. Twenty minutes of the two hours had gone by already. He sprinted to the munitions shack as best he could, still breathing through the scuba gear. Everything he needed was in the shack. He had plastic explosives, not C4 but probably almost as reliable. He found timers, radio-controlled electronic servo-mechanisms, detonators, and cartons of TNT, probably a ton of the stuff.

He worked quickly. In minutes he had charges set to blow in two and a half hours: an hour and a half for the personnel to get out alive and another hour for the whole thing to blow.

Satisfied, Carter moved back to the sub as quickly as possible. This time he had more trouble getting into the air lock with his new burden.

Before he untied the Russians, he held a surprise in front of their faces. He'd fashioned two belts for them, both radio-controlled. He locked the belts in place, each stuffed with a pound of plastic explosive, then released their bonds.

"I have two radio controls here, servo-mechanisms to delight any scientist. They will spread you over the walls of this sub like raspberry jam.

"An interesting problem for a scientist," he went on. "If I seal this sub and use its internal radio link, will my radio control work from outside? If it works, will the internal pressure the explosion creates blow the seams and send the sub to the bottom?

"I think it will," Carter concluded.

"You devil!" Vilitchin shouted.

"An angel compared to your people. Have you ever been to the Serbsky Institute, comrade? Have you met the ones who specialize in torture and interrogation?" Carter asked. "Not a nice place at all. The specialists there make me look like a saint."

"What do you want from us?" Gregarov asked, his voice giving away his fear and acceptance.

"Ah, a pragmatist," Carter said, grinning. "I need some work from you and some information."

"And if you get it?" Gregarov asked.

"A full pardon. You would have to be debriefed, of course. But I can see the information you have giving you a ticket to freedom."

"Defection?" Gregarov asked.

"No! We will not defect. It is impossible!" Vilitchin said, his voice unsteady, almost hysterical.

"This is not a deal for you, comrade," Carter said.

"No defections for idealists. Besides, you are not a valuable commodity. No use to us at all."

"What do you want?" Gregarov asked.

"Who was behind this project? I want his name," Carter said.

"I spoke to him today. General Protopopoff. Head of the First Chief Directorate."

"You are a traitor!" Vilitchin screamed. He was a chubby young man who apparently seldom bathed. In the confines of the submarine his body odor was almost overpowering.

Carter glanced at his watch. He had an hour before the personnel in the cavern woke up and he had a lot more work to do and little time to do it.

"Who are the replacements your young friend spoke of?" Carter asked Gregarov.

"I forbid you to tell him!" Vilitchin shrieked, sweat running down his round face and off his chin.

"The military man in charge is Captain Persov. He asked the general for a replacement for my assistant, Valeri Berof. I know of no others," Gregarov said. "But I wouldn't be surprised if the general sent in some other experts. He was very upset by your infiltration."

"Who was Berof? You didn't like him, did you?" Carter asked. He had noted the distaste when Gregarov spoke the name. Petty likes and dislikes made for enemies. Or perhaps Berof was a watchdog.

"He was KGB, a full colonel—" Gregarov started to say.

"I will kill you!" Vilitchin shouted. "When I get out of this I will kill you!"

Carter backhanded the man across the face. "Shut up, you fool. I didn't want to kill you, but you are forcing my hand. Now, keep out of it." He turned to Gregarov. "Go ahead, comrade. Full colonels are not usually watchdogs for projects like this. What was he doing here?''

Gregarov looked tired and uncertain. He was a man of little strength and no tolerance for pain. It was not difficult to see he would go on as long as he thought it would save his life. ''He was observing Margate,'' he said. ''The Squire had been here for so long, Berof didn't trust him. Few of us trusted him. He seemed so like the people we were trying to destroy.''

Carter thought about what he'd learned for a minute. ''I have several things to do in the cavern,'' he said. ''Can you make this submarine ready for sea by yourself?''

''Yes. I don't need this sniveling ball of fat,'' the small Russian sneered.

Carter secured Vilitchin's hands and feet again and left Gregarov's free. ''Then get started,'' he said. ''One other thing. We will call your General Protopopoff, comrade. When I return, we will call the general. I'm not sure what I want to say to him, but you'd better remember the codes to get to him. Without them, I'm going to have to send you on a long trip to hell with your chubby friend. Is that clear?'' Carter finished in perfect Russian.

''It is.''

''Good.''

Carter looked at his watch. Forty minutes before the first of them recovered from the effects of the gas. Time. The goddamned time! He had so much to do before then.

FIFTEEN

With only minutes to go until the effect of the gas wore off, Carter didn't even check his watch as he made his way past sprawled bodies to the communications room. He had to find a way to get the scores of men out of the cavern before it blew.

To the average man, the communications room would have looked like something out of the next century. Fortunately for Carter, AXE's specialist in all things mechanical and electronic had recently taken him through the latest developments. He bypassed all the sophisticated hardware in search of a simple recorded message mechanism that he could put on the public address system.

The PA system wasn't difficult to find. At the one desk in the room, located so the communications chief could look down on the floor of the cavern through a massive plate glass window, a microphone on a swivel was placed over the center of the desk's surface. Next to it, a recording machine with a separate microphone and special tape was already set up for broadcast of continuous messages.

Carter pushed the play button. The recording boomed out at the prone bodies in the cavern:

"*. . . Attention. Attention. All personnel will report for orientation on the new diving bell. A schedule is posted on the bulletin board. You will read the notice* *and conform immediately."*

Carter didn't try to improve on the style. If that's what they were accustomed to, that's what they would get. He thumbed the record button and lifted the small recording microphone to his mouth:

". . . Attention. Attention. Bombs have been placed in the work areas by enemy agents. You will evacuate through the upper entrance immediately."

He used the same inflections and tried to make his Russian sound as similar to the other message's as possible. He pushed the rewind and play buttons and listened to the first playthrough. The message would be repeated every thirty seconds.

Conscious of the time, Carter scrambled back to the sub and his captives. Gregarov was at work on the final stages of starting up the small craft. In a few minutes they would take her below the surface and out to the middle of the bay. Vilitchin was still bound, glaring at Gregarov with undisguised hatred and now at Carter with the same heated emotion. His eyes were all he could use to express himself. Carter didn't trust the man to move about the sub. He kept him bound and gagged until he would need him when they started to move.

"How's it going?" he asked Gregarov.

"We can start engines in a few minutes."

"Okay. Leave it for a minute. Show me the communications center on this tub."

Gregarov led the way through narrow steel companionways past the men's sleeping quarters and to a cubbyhole of a room aft. He squeezed behind the desk, switched on a powerful radio, and coded in a series of numbers. As he worked, Carter memorized every move.

"North Sea Command," a voice came through the overhead speaker sounding metallic and weak.

Gregarov turned a couple of dials to improve the

sound. "Patch me into KGB headquarters," he commanded, "the First Chief Directorate switchboard."

"Identify."

"Yuri Gregarov, chief of research, Project Cavern. Identity: National Academy of Science codes, Able Baker Zebra two-zero-zero-two-one."

"Wait." The command was curt, probably from a frustrated junior clerk thousands of miles away and isolated by layers of security.

"First Chief Directorate." A female voice came at them unexpectedly, loud and clear.

Gregarov repeated the identity codes. "I must speak to General Protopopoff. He ordered me to call him with any new development."

"Wait." The command was the same as the first but with a little more warmth.

"We have to get him on the move," Carter warned. "Make sure he's sufficiently alarmed to act fast."

"The general will talk to you. Wait," another voice commanded.

They waited. Carter looked at his watch. Ten minutes until the men started waking and that was accurate to within ten percent.

"Yes, Gregarov. What is so damned important?"

"Comrade General. We are still having trouble here. Comrade Margate was temporarily captured. We rescued him but he was wounded." Gregarov was sweating, confined in the small steel box of a room. The sweat was partly from fear.

"You have been compromised. I will not permit this project to fail. How do you plan to cover the exposure, Gregarov?" the angry general asked.

"This is not my area of expertise. I am a scientist, General," Gregarov said, his voice almost a whine. "If I may suggest, only the very best you have can turn this around. Perhaps you could come . . . ?''

The other end of the line was silent. Gregarov and Carter waited while the general thought it over. Carter had put a pair of earphones on his head to study the general's voice better. For further reference, he had turned on a recording device.

"Very well. I will come," the general finally said.

"Pardon, General," Gregarov asked, his voice that of a supplicant. "You mentioned others on the way. May I ask who they are and when they will arrive?"

"You may not. They are very important members of my team. If this were not of the highest priority, I would let them clean it up."

"And they will arrive . . . ?"

"They are there by now. With Comrade Margate."

"I'm pleased you will be coming, General. I have not felt confident about the future of the project until now."

"Yes. Well, I'll be there as fast as I can. This is top secret, Gregarov. It would be disastrous if I fell into enemy hands. As it is, the premier may have my head for leaving the country."

"You will be a hero of the Soviet Union, General."

"I already am, you fool. And I'm jeopardizing everything I've achieved for this."

"You won't be sorry, General," Gregarov said but found he was talking to a dead line.

Carter could see the doubt on the small Russian's face. He hadn't realized until now the enormity of what he had done. This was a bonus for Carter. His plan was to have the general out of the way and to have a recording of his voice. To learn he was going to visit the country was a coup worth more than destroying Margate and this whole project combined.

"Go ahead with your work, Gregarov," Carter

ordered. "I want to listen to that voice again."

When the scientist had gone, Carter played the tape over and over until he had familiarized himself with the voice. Then he dialed Margate's house across the bay.

"Yes," a voice said without any form of identification.

"This is General Protopopoff. Get the Squire for me," Carter commanded, imitating the general's voice well enough to scare an underling.

"Yes, sir."

Soon another voice came on. "General. This is Captain Persov. Comrade Margate has been wounded. He is being treated right now," the young military man said, his tone giving away the condition of his shattered nerves.

"Captain"—Carter spit out the title with venom—"I don't care if he is on his deathbed. I will speak with him, not underlings. Now!"

The line was quiet for a full two minutes. Carter sweated in the confines of the small room. Not because of the subterfuge he was into, but because of the time. He had a plan. And he had to return to the entrance once again to make it work. He had to run the gauntle of the cavern personnel all the way from the sub to the top and back.

"Margate." It was a different Margate who answered, not the voice of the man Carter had heard before when the man was on top and in control. It was the voice of a defeated Margate, weak and near the end.

"General Protopopoff. It has been reported to me that the project is finished. Is that correct, Comrade Margate?"

"No, sir. A temporary setback. That is all. Temporary," the voice said weakly.

"You don't sound strong enough to command,"

arter said, imitating the Russian general to perfection.

"I can handle it, General."

"Have the people I sent arrived?"

"It was not necessary. I can handle it."

"I doubt that very much. Now, here is what you will o," Carter said, the steel in his voice brooking no argument. "You will take all the people I sent you and proed to the cavern. You will create order out of the haos that I've been told exists there now. You will remain there until I arrive."

"You arrive? But—"

Carter took great satisfaction in hanging up in the iddle of Margate's confusion. It gave him satisfaction nd it gave him time. He had one more thing to do.

He rushed to the control room, past the two Russians, nd was about to leave, when a thought occurred to im. "Is she ready?" he asked Gregarov.

"Yes."

He stopped to tie up the small Russian once more. He anted the sub to be there when he got back. When he as finished, he took off at a trot. He discarded the cuba gear and headed for the communications room gain.

Some of the Russians were beginning to stir. It was a armless gas and they would all fully recover. They ight be groggy for the first few minutes, but they ould have full command of their faculties soon.

In the communications center Carter looked on the helves of supplies for what he wanted. He found a pair f powerful communicators, long-range walkie-talkies, nd tested them for sensitivity. Satisfied, he started to he top of the cavern again, weaving his way past restess bodies, some standing, uncertainly, holding their eads.

At the entrance, he set one of the communicators

behind a rock and turned it on with the volume on high. He started back only to find some of the Russians standing alertly, looking at him questioningly.

"*. . . Attention. Attention. Bombs have been placed in the work areas by enemy agents. You will evacuate through the upper entrance immediately.*"

The recorded announcement boomed through the cavern sounding very official, similar to the one he'd tried to copy.

The Russians turned their attention from him and headed like robots for the entrance. Carter continued to the lower level, sometimes bumping into Russians now starting to panic as they'd heard the announcement a half-dozen times.

As he neared the sub, two guards, completely recovered and with their Kalashnikovs held at the ready barred his path.

Carter jumped to one side behind a workbench as the Russians opened up, then took a quick look at his watch. The countdown for the explosion was less than forty-five minutes. He didn't have much time left to indulge in firefights.

The slugs from the AK-47s whined off steel as they hit the bench and took off at odd angles to chip at the stone of the walls. A steady hail of fire kept Carter pinned down until he heard the firing pins of the two guns click against empty chambers.

His 9mm Luger was in his hand. He looked around the bench and fired twice. One of the guards was caught in the open. His face was frozen in an expression of horror as his body crumpled to the floor.

The other guard was out of sight. Carter could hear him snap a new magazine into his gun. The man was behind a rock to the left of the dead man.

Carter stood his ground, Wilhelmina ready. The Ru

sian would not be able to sight his weapon and fire before the Luger spat death at him.

Time was the enemy. A full minute passed. At last the Russian sprang from hiding, the Kalashnikov spitting its small missiles high over Carter's head. As the guard tried to bring the weapon to bear on the man in black, two holes appeared in his head and he went down.

Carter holstered his weapon and leaped for the sub as fast as his legs could carry him across the rough ground at the bottom of the cavern.

Inside, Gregarov was glaring at him like a trapped animal. The man had thought that because he had capitulated, Carter would trust him. The Russian was like the most naïve of men when it came to the facts of life. The thought occurred to Carter, as he untied the small man, that Gregarov should have stayed in his laboratory in Moscow.

"Let's get under way," Carter ordered.

"You cannot treat me like this. I was willing to cooperate," the man complained, "but—"

"This is war," Carter said to him angrily. "Perhaps the fact escaped you." He flipped his stiletto into his right hand and held it at the Russian's throat.

Gregarov's eyes bulged at the sight of the sharp steel blade. "I will need Vilitchin to help me," he croaked.

"To do what?" Carter asked.

"I will be at the periscope. I need someone to steer," the small Russian said, his composure partially restored.

Carter untied the squirming Vilitchin.

"I will kill you before this day is over," the young man snarled.

Carter had combined the two radio controls into one. He waved the small black box at the young Russian, pointing to the body bomb both Russians wore. "You will never know what hit you," he said.

"I've given that some thought, American," Vilitchin said. "You will never use it. Not while you are on the sub." He stood grinning at Carter, not moving to perform his task.

"Perhaps you are right." Carter turned on him with the stiletto and in a flash had slashed at both cheeks until blood ran off the Russian's chin. "Now we will get under way," he ordered.

He looked at his watch. A half hour had passed since he had talked to Margate and it was a half hour until the cavern blew.

Gregarov turned on a switch and waited for the surge that would tell him the atomic pile was transferring its power to the propellers.

"It's not working," he said.

"I remind you that if we do not get under way, we will go up with the cavern in a half hour. *Now let's get the hell out of here!*" Carter shouted.

Slowly the sub began to reverse out of the narrow channel that formed the entrance to the cave. It took five minutes to clear the entrance and change from reverse to foward motion. In another five minutes they were a hundred yards from the entrance and well under way.

"I'm going to the radio room. If you try anything, you will die immediately. I have little use for you now if you don't cooperate," he said as he turned to the rear of the small ship.

In the radio room, he used the powerful radio to reach AXE's communications center. He gave his codes and was patched into Hawk's position.

"Where are you now?" he asked his chief.

"At the entrance. We've rounded up the Russians."

"Then get the hell out. You've got about twenty minutes," Carter said.

"We've got them all?" Hawk asked.

"Not quite. Margate and a few VIP Russians are headed for the cavern right now. Let them get inside and don't let them see your people."

"Okay. The evacuation is complete. Where the hell are *you*?" Hawk asked.

"In one of the subs headed out to the center of the bay."

"Won't the shock waves from the explosion catch you out there?"

"Don't think so. It should blow straight up. And we'll be far enough out in time."

"So why did you call? We were on our way and you already asked us to let Margate and his people past."

"A new score. Protopopoff is on his way to supervise personally," Carter said, knowing the thought had brought a huge smile to the face of the older man at the other end of the line.

"I'll blanket the place. I'll get MI5 on it." Hawk sounded like a kid with a new toy.

"Get the hell out of the way first. Remember, you owe me a dinner at the Dorchester."

Carter hung up, starting to reflect on the capture of the powerful KGB general, when the noises he had been waiting for sounded through the communicator he had set up at the mouth of the cavern. It was Margate's voice talking to several others.

"*Where is everyone? It is so quiet. Come, we must inspect the offices and the subs. Watch out for booby traps . . .*"

The voices receded to the bowels of the cavern. Carter looked at his watch. Ten minutes until his charges blew.

Suddenly a scream tore through the metal companionways. Carter ran for the control room to find Vilitchin standing over Gregarov's body. Vilitchin had run the small man against the bulkhead until Gregarov's head was a bloody pulp. The floor and the walls of the control room nearby were speckled with red.

The young Russian turned to Carter. He held the steering control in his hand as a weapon.

Carter flipped Hugo into his palm, took the blade between thumb and finger in one fluid motion, and threw the knife. It sliced cleanly through the man's throat until only the hilt was showing. Vilitchin looked surprised. It took almost ten seconds for his knees to buckle and his face to crash into the steel mesh floor of the room.

Carter raced to the periscope. He swung it to the shore and focused on the cliff surface. He checked the compass heading. The sub's prow was pointed straight for the cliff at twenty knots.

Carter lunged for the wheel that controlled the steering mechanism. He pried it from Vilitchin's hand and tried to turn it back on its shaft.

It was a straight shaft, not a threaded one. A steel key was needed to hold the wheel firmly to the shaft. Vilitchin had thrown the key away.

Carter looked at the time.

If his watch and the timers were coordinated, he had only five minutes until the cavern blew.

He shut down the power and felt the ship wallow as her backwash surfed her toward the entrance to the cavern.

SIXTEEN

Carter had so little time. He was trapped inside a steel shell, partially submerged. Two men lay dead in their own blood in the control room. And the cavern was set to blow in a matter of seconds.

He thought of swimming out in scuba gear, but the pressure of the explosion bursting from the entrance would toss him far out to sea and the concussion would probably kill him.

Trying to keep his nerves from snapping and his mind functioning, he searched the ship as quickly as he could. He had to come up with an idea.

The rescue apparatus. What if he . . . ?

Carter picked up two inflatable dinghies still in their plastic containers and headed for the captain's tiny cubicle. He dumped the inflatables on the bunk and headed back to the supply locker. He picked out a fresh tank of air and a mask, complete with breathing apparatus, and he was ready for an undersea escape if the sub survived the explosion.

The last item he kept with him was the radio control for the explosives still strapped to the two Russians.

The room was so small he had a great deal of trouble maneuvering the equipment he needed. He closed the door and twisted the half-dozen lugs that sealed the small room off from the rest of the boat.

He looked at his watch. One minute to zero hour.

Maybe he would make it if he didn't run into any snags.

Carter slipped into the scuba gear.

Thirty seconds left.

He took the plastic wrappers off the new inflatable dinghies and positioned them on each side of him.

He pulled the plugs on the inflators. Sealed in the small room, the only thing he could hear was the hiss of gas as it filled the rubber boats.

As he felt himself lifted off his feet and crushed between the two forces, he began to wonder if he had designed his own manner of death. Just as the two balloonlike boats filled every corner of the room, holding the man between them, the pressure stopped. He was still able to breathe.

As if the holocaust he had created in the cavern had waited for him, he heard a dull roar and the room started to turn in violent somersaults like a child's toy boat caught in a violent sea.

Geremy Farnsworth Margate had lost little of his aplomb as he led the visitors from Moscow to inspect the project that was General Protopopoff's pride and joy. He was dressed in the newest of his Savile Row suits, a neat sling securing his wounded shoulder.

No one was in the cavern. No one.

He turned to the men with him to offer an explanation, but the words died on his lips. He made a futile gesture with his one good hand. He had no explanation to offer.

What greeted him as he turned were the stern faces of the chiefs of the Second and Third Departments of the First Chief Directorate, two of the general's most trusted men. With them was the head of the National Academy of Science. They had aides with them, younger men, the real workers, the men who supplied the detailed answers for most situations. They were the ones who would compose the final report on Project Cavern that would end up on the general's desk.

Captain Persov trailed behind.

"I don't know, comrades. I just don't know," Margate said, his face beginning to show his complete bewilderment. "Gregarov should have been here to greet us."

The PA system ground out a message, but the security people had the speakers close to the entrance turned low and the sound came at them like a ghostly voice, far away and indistinct.

"Where are your men, Persov?" Margate demanded as he continued to lead them into the depths of the deserted cavern.

"I don't know, comrade. It is as much a puzzle to me as to you."

"It is your business to know, Persov! I'm beginning to wonder if you can fill Lobanov's shoes," Margate said. He had to vent his anger on someone and Persov was the only one available.

They continued further into the cavern, the recorded message blaring out from the speakers below, indistinct and with a hollow sound where they walked up above.

"Listen!" one of the VIPs said. "The announcement. Is it a warning?" he asked.

The recording could be heard indistinctly every thirty seconds. As they rounded a corner, they came closer to the engineering office structure and the munitions shack. A speaker blasted the message out loud and clear.

"*. . . Attention. Attention. Bombs have been placed in the work areas by enemy agents. You will evacuate through the upper entrance immediately.*"

"That's why my men have disappeared," Persov

said, stunned. "But where have they gone? Why are they not searching for the bombs?"

"Rats leaving the ship. Who the hell cares?" the chief of the Second Department shouted. "Let's get the hell out of here!" He turned and started to run for the exit, knocking Persov off his feet in his haste.

The rest all turned as one and started to run, leaving Persov on the ground, bewildered and bleeding where the stone had peeled back the skin from his hands.

As they ran, the announcement came again:

". . . *Attention. Attention. Bombs have been placed in the work areas by enemy agents. You will evacuate through the upper . . .*"

The munitions shack blew.

The force of the explosion could go only two ways. The shack was on a stone floor and against a solid stone wall, so the force went straight out and up.

The crushing force of air and debris caught the small group of Russians and flung them against the far wall of the cavern, crushing every bone and sending the wasted bodies upward in a funnel of power that took the roof off the cavern and sent skyward every particle it could tear loose.

Everything that went up floated earthward eventually, but not in any form that was recognizable.

A second direction took the rest of the blast. The force that couldn't find its way through the upper opening, pushed its way, in a fraction of a second, to the entrance below. It took the two submarines closest to the entrance, crushed them against the rock opening, enlarging it, then threw them out to sea, crushed beyond recognition, in a wall of water that was big enough to challenge any created by Mother Nature at her worst.

• • •

David Hawk had moved away from the immediate vicinity of the explosion. He stood at the tip of Greenstone Point and looked out at Gruinard Bay. From long experience, he knew the charges Carter had set would explode out the entrance and through the roof.

His immediate concern was for Carter. He had trained his binoculars on the sub as it left the entrance. He had been amazed to see the steel hull turn and head back toward the entrance.

That could mean only one thing. Carter was not in control and he was in trouble. The man who had been his prize agent for years was in a small sub heading back the wrong way.

The sub faltered, and when the props stopped turning, it seemed to coast back to the cavern entrance on its own backwash.

Hawk looked at his watch. Fifteen seconds passed . . . and another five.

Then she blew.

As he watched, the top blew off the cavern taking the surface of the cliff with it, including a farm, its outbuildings, and an old Bedford truck.

The chief of AXE was stunned by the power of the upward force. He watched in awe as the outward explosion at sea level enlarged the opening of the cavern and set up a wave the height of a five-story building.

Then the pressure of the blast hit him. He was knocked off his feet and skidded across the rocky surface over the harsh growth of wild juniper and bramble.

The veteran of espionage wars beyond counting crawled to the edge of the cliff, cut and bleeding in a dozen places. He was just in time to see the huge wave pick up the sub and tumble it bow after stern, end over

end, out to sea, until he lost sight of the wreck as it was
lost among the froth and flotsam in the wake of the
monster wave.

Carter rode the bouncing hulk as it was tossed amid
other debris out to sea. Pressed between the two inflatables, he was totally disoriented. Up and down, left
and right, direction no longer meant anything. Locked
in the darkness of his prison, he knew only motion and
sound.

The motion went on interminably. The sound was of
water on a steel hull, smashed hard by resisting water,
dulled by the cocoon of inflated rubber. It was like
going over a mammoth falls in a barrel. He had often
thought the men who tried it had a death wish, that they
were sure to die. As the motion continued . . . and the
sound . . . on and on . . . he was sure he was a dead man.

Soldiers had come to the pub at Poolewe to warn the
locals about the impending explosion, but Brodie and
the rest of them had refused to budge. The captain of
the militia unit was a fisherman turned oilman from Inverness and he couldn't get them to move. Finally, he
had reported in to his major and left them to their own
fate.

"What do you suppose is going on now?" Jack
Brodie asked no one in particular.

"Carter said he was going to blow the damned place.
I say good luck to him," one of the old men said, raising
his glass.

"But why would they want to evacuate us? The
damned place is miles away," another speculated.

"The only reason could be nuclear. I been reading
about the protests in France and Germany. Do you suppose they could have put some nuclear bombs down

there?'' Maggie Brodie asked.

"Don't be daft, woman,'' Brodie said. "Nuclear bombs would take out the whole coast.''

"That's what I was thinking. The whole coast,'' she said.

The room was silent for a few minutes as the men contemplated their mugs and thought private thoughts.

"Jock was the fifth to go. The sixth counting that aviator fellow,'' one of the sheep men said. "Damn me if that's not a bloody war now.

"First there was the young lad,'' he went on. "Then we lost Old Alf. Then that Geoff fellow. He wasn't such a bad sort, you know?''

"What about the woman?'' Brodie asked. "A bad bunch to kill the woman.''

"Did you see her?'' one asked. "Ready for battle she was. Professional. I wonder if she got some of the bastards before they got her.''

A foreign noise attacked their ears. A *vroom* that seemed to lift the inn from its solid stone foundation and sent freshly washed glass mugs skidding to the floor behind the bar. The sound of the explosion was followed by the sound of broken glass, then a wind like the breath of the devil shook the old building.

The men were silent. Maggie managed to hold back a scream.

Then, as a man, they bolted for the door and took off across the barren moors to the cliffside at Greenstone Point.

The steel hull was no longer cartwheeling through the water. Carter knew the sub was free from the wave that had engulfed it, but he didn't know what condition it was in. The hull could be split and they could be heading for the bottom. All the hatches could be sprung and impossible to open. He had no way of knowing.

Slowly, the pressure of the inflated rubber fighting against him, he managed to free his stiletto and grasp it awkwardly in his right hand. At first he couldn't get the point near the rubber. Finally he forced the point against the rubber and waited.

If he punctured one dinghy, would the other throw him against the far bulkhead? What would happen to the compressed air that escaped? He made sure the scuba mouthpiece was in place and the air valve turned on.

Then he pushed the knife harder into the inflatable until it exploded beside him.

Carter was smashed against the far wall, spraining his right shoulder. The excess air escaped through a ventilating duct set in the ceiling.

Massaging his right shoulder for a minute, Carter sat in the darkness and waited to compose himself. If he was at the bottom of Gruinard Bay, how deep was it? Could he get back to the surface? He looked at his diving watch. He had twenty minutes of air left. Twenty minutes to free himself from the cabin, to escape the submarine, and to get to the surface.

He slashed at the second dinghy with the sharp point of his knife and withstood the shock of compressed air better the second time. Too bad he'd had to use them. The two dinghies were the only ones in the supply locker. One of them would have been useful on the surface . . . if he ever made it to the surface.

He hesitated to turn the six lugs that would free him from the cabin. If the sub was on the bottom, water would rush in. He loosed the lugs one at a time, then braced himself against the steel bunk as he turned the door handle.

A small amount of water trickled in. He couldn't see

it in the blackness of the cabin, but he would feel it against his rubber-coated feet. He could also hear the seawater. It was no more than a trickle as it filled the floor of the cabin.

Carter reached down with one gloved hand. He could feel seven or eight inches of water. Okay. He knew he could live with that. He pulled off the mouthpiece and sampled the air. It was stale but life-supporting. So he turned off the air valve to conserve what he had. Before he left the room, he felt around for the radio control in its waterproof plastic container and tied it to his waist.

Every inch of the interior was pitch-black. Carter had no light and he didn't know where to find one. He remembered to turn left toward the control room. It was less than five minutes from the time he'd punctured the inflatables to the moment his foot struck a corpse that floated in the shallow water.

Carter stepped over one body, then the other. At first he ignored them, but then he went back and lifted them in the dark and carried them to bunks in the crew's quarters. He might want them dry later on.

Back in the control room, he felt around for the periscope and the eyepieces.

The periscope was out of the water! He could see a part of the coastline. It was far away. He estimated the wave had carried him out more than seven miles. But the sub was afloat and that was something.

It was great to be able to see something light. When he turned from the periscope, all was dark again and he had to grope to find his way.

The conning tower was to the left of the periscope. As he remembered, it was about fifteen feet. He slipped and fell twice in the short space between the periscope and the conning tower, but there was no way he could avoid it. The place was filled with controls, some jutting from the walls, others from the ceiling. Before he found the conning tower, he had cracked his head twice against an obstacle and he'd smashed his diving glasses.

The hatch was stuck shut. No way was he going to get out that way, he realized.

If only he could see what he was doing. He lowered himself down the ladder from the conning tower and sat on a bench in the dark, thinking.

What the hell had the damned subs looked like in the cavern? What had they looked like in dry dock? He cursed himself for not having made a full inspection before he set the charges. It wasn't like him to forget to cover his retreat. But everything happened so fast. He'd had so little time.

The plexiglass observation room he'd seen!

That was it. But where the hell was it? Below the control room? At water level when the superstructure towered over it? How did one get to it?

He tried feeling all along the wall at the base of the conning tower without success. His foot struck a latch and an opening began to show in front of him. The pneumatics had quit along with the power. Carter fought the door open with brute strength.

Everything below was filled with water. He tried to look down, but all he could see was a wall of water and dim light coming from the other end of the room below.

The sub was barely afloat. She was a good ten feet lower in the water than normal.

He'd have to use his precious scuba air. So be it. If he didn't explore the area below, he wasn't going to get out of the tub anyway.

He adjusted the mouthpiece, tested, and without a face mask, slipped below into the observation room. He couldn't see clearly without his mask. With the sight he had and by touch, he quickly learned the room had no escape hatch.

He found a group of drawers and rummaged through them. One contained an underwater flashlight.

At last Lady Luck had given him the slightest of glances. Maybe she would look his way and he'd find an air lock and get the hell out of this place.

He dived further and came up at the back of the ship. He climbed a set of steel rungs and found himself in the back of the supply closet. A diving mask was the first thing his light shone on.

Now he could see clearly. He checked his watch. Only ten minutes of air left. Ten minutes to find an air lock and force it open.

Tools. The supply room had tools. He found hammers of all weights and some crowbars. Just what he needed when he found the air lock. He selected one of each and slipped them under his belt.

Last, he found two tanks of air. Relief flooded through him as he approached them. With these babies he'd have at least eighty minutes of air and in that time he'd be sure to find an exit.

He shone the flashlight on the first tank.

Empty.

He was almost afraid to check the second tank. Surely the Russians couldn't be so stupid. They'd have to keep a fresh supply on each sub at all times.

The second one was empty too.

He looked at his watch again.

Four minutes and counting.

SEVENTEEN

The men had followed Jack Brodie to the edge of the cliff. They arrived too late to see anything. David Hawk was standing not far from them, scraped and bruised from his tumble across the rocky ground when the cavern blew.

"What happened to that Carter fellow?" Jack Brodie asked.

"He's in a small submarine blown out to sea," Hawk said, surprised at the question. These men were not the enemy. They were locals. "You know him?" he asked.

"Our mate. He went after the buggers by himself," Brodie said. "He did it for us. Is he alive?" he asked.

"It's possible," Hawk answered. "The sub took one hell of a beating. If he was tumbled around inside it, he couldn't have made it. But he's got more lives than a dozen cats. I just don't know."

"Then let's find out," Brodie said, leaving the oldest of the men sitting on boulders, still winded, as he raced back to town. Two of the younger ones followed him.

"Where's he going?" Hawk asked the old men who had not followed.

"Fraser's boat, if it's still there. You could catch 'em at the Brig o' Ewe, the bridge in the middle of town."

Hawk set out for the town as fast as his condition would allow. He could see Brodie in the distance.

• • •

Carter finned through the water along the companionway to the plexiglass in the bow. He jammed his light in a steel rack, pointing at the thick plastic window. Two swivel seats were installed close to the plastic. He sat in one and pulled the hammer and crowbar from his belt. He had kept the servo-mechanism with him, the radio control to blow the explosives that were strapped to the dead Russians.

His watch showed no air left in his tank. For the last few breaths he had felt a difference. Less oxygen. He began to feel light-headed. If he swam back to the control room, he would find air, enough for a few hours. But he would not find a way out.

Hawk arrived at the bridge in time to see Brodie and the other two head Fraser's diesel-powered boat, the one Carter had used, toward the sea. He waved at them, climbed over the abutment of the bridge, and hung down, holding on with one arm and signaling to them with the other.

"Hold up! Wait for me!" he shouted.

At the helm, Brodie swung the bow over while the other two caught Hawk as they came up to the rusted old steel and concrete bridge. As Hawk let go, the three of them fell to the bottom of the boat, Hawk on top. It wasn't a maneuver designed for men their age.

Brodie's attention was on the white water ahead. He steered for a channel, and unlike Carter's efforts when the Killmaster was more interested in stealth, opened up the old diesel and made fifteen knots with the current. Once at sea, in the swells of Gruinard Bay, he knew that with his best effort he wasn't going to get to the sub's position for almost an hour.

• • •

Carter had swung the hammer scores of times and hadn't as much as chipped the plastic window. With his breathing becoming labored and his chest sore, fighting for air, he put the crowbar in one corner and used the hammer to force it around a solid rubber grommet.

After three tries, he could finally see some space between the bar and the hull. He pulled the bar sideways with all his strength. The bar was slightly curved and allowed him some leverage. He put the hammer, one with a ten-pound head and a long handle, under the crowbar to form a fulcrum, and pulled with all the strength he had left.

The plastic began to peel away from the hull. He could see two inches of daylight . . . then six . . . then a dozen. Carter reached down for the edge of the plastic and peeled it from the rubber grommet until it all came away in one strong, curved sheet.

He was free. He dropped the tools, clipped the plastic box containing the radio mechanism to his belt, and finned through the open observation port.

He was not ten feet below the surface. He scissored his feet to take him up, his vision blurred by lack of oxygen. Just as he reached the surface, the image behind his eyes turned to blue, almost like a daylight sky but dotted with bright stars. Another few seconds and the blue would have turned to black—the final curtain.

Carter reached the surface and tore off his mouthpiece. He gulped for air—blessed pure, clean life-giving air.

While he peeled the tank from his back and let it fall, he looked shoreward. He could see the cavern far away at the base of the cliffs. The hole was a lot bigger. He could see that even from a distance.

So they were dead. The leaders were dead and the others were in custody by now. He rolled over onto his back, free of the scuba gear but tired. He was too tired to swim seven or eight miles without a rest. He knew he could float on his back for an hour, then make it to the nearest shore.

As he let the three-foot swell roll him gently in its re-lentless motion, he thought he heard a voice calling. It sounded like Hawk. Impossible. He might be halluci-nating. Yet it could be. Though Hawk normally stayed in his office to direct operations, this time he was in the United Kingdom. He'd been with the troops near the cliffs. It was entirely possible that he was nearby.

Carter flipped to his stomach so he could crane his head. At the crest of each rolling swell, he looked for Hawk, for a boat, for any craft between himself and the shore.

He saw it! Fraser's old hulk was bearing down on him. He waved as best he could. They were beside him in minutes.

Carter was hauled over the gunwales and deposited on the floor of the cockpit.

Hawk was grinning at him, an unlit stogie stuck in the corner of his mouth. "You okay, Nick?" he asked.

"I'm all right," Carter responded, grinning back.

"The cavern is finished, Nick," Hawk said, holding nothing back, knowing instinctively the men in the boat knew most of it. "Somehow we've got to scuttle the sub."

"Why not let her go, mate? Be a great catch for the Royal Navy," Brodie suggested.

"Believe me when I tell you it would be better at the bottom of the sea," Hawk said. "Think we can manage it, Nick? Can we board her and set some charges?"

"No need," Carter said, handing him the plastic box.

Hawk knew what the radio control was. "Is she wired?" he asked.

"She's wired," Carter said, without going into details. He had faced the fact that the sub had to be sunk to erase all evidence of Project Cavern. But he didn't stomach the idea of using the two dead men to do it.

Hawk opened the box and flipped the switch. A red light glowed on the front of the panel. He handed the box to Brodie. "Maybe you'd like to do it," he said kindly.

This was unprecedented for Hawk. Carter had never seen him acknowledge a civilian in an operation, much less hand one a detonator. They must have struck up a bond in one hell of a hurry.

"My pleasure," Brodie said, smiling, and Hawk showed him how to push the button.

The sub seemed to rise slightly out of the water. Bubbles escaped from her in a rush of foam. When the bubbles began to clear, the periscope was gone and so was the conning tower.

She was on her way to the bottom.

"Let's get back," Hawk said.

"Back to the pub," Brodie suggested. "Maggie will be worried."

"Drinks are on the house," he added.

His old customers just stared, then looked at each other, too dumbfounded to talk. They hadn't expected to live to hear the words.

DON'T MISS THE NEXT NEW
NICK CARTER SPY THRILLER

NIGHT OF THE CONDOR

The guard shack provided the perfect blind for keeping the street under surveillance. The size of four phone booths combined, it was topped by a slanted roof. The side facing the pier was open, its door having fallen off at the hinges. The other three walls each had a narrow window, supplying vantage points.

Inside the shack was a table and two chairs. Carter positioned a chair so he could see through all three slitlike windows.

He sat down and waited for his guests.

They arrived at three o'clock.

A light blue van cruised slowly down the street. Carter ducked down and watched it over the top of the windowsill.

The van entered the yard, reversed, and backed into a spot diagonally across from the shack. A wall of barrels hid it from the street. It faced outward for a quick getaway.

The engine shut off and Vasquez and Yavar got out

of the cab. Even in the weak light of a cloudy day, Yavar looked pale and pasty.

Vasquez pounded on the wall of the van. Its rear door opened and two men got out.

They looked tough and competent. One carried an automatic rifle loaded with a banana clip. The other cradled an M-1 machine pistol in his arms.

The machine gunner asked, "What do we do now?"

"We wait," Vasquez said.

"If Carter's smart, he'll get here early," Yavar said.

"If he's smart, he'll stay away."

"He thinks he's got us fooled, but he'll find out who's the fool." Yavar consulted his wristwatch. "You men will get into position by four o'clock. As soon as Carter's inside, cut him down."

"I hope we don't have to wait too long," the youth said.

"Why don't we take him alive?" Vasquez suggested. "That way we could have some fun with him before we kill him."

"Nothing fancy. Just shoot him and be done with it," Yavar said. "Besides, the man is tricky. Look at how he handled Tanango last night."

"I wish I could have seen that," the machine gunner said and grinned.

"Too bad Tanango's not along on the job," Yellow Shirt said. "I bet he'd like to pay that *yanqui* bastard back for spoiling his face."

"Don't waste your time feeling sorry for Tanango. He's the lucky one. He gets to take care of that treacherous Brazilian bitch," Vasquez informed them.

They all broke up laughing.

That changed everything. Carter had planned to wait until the group separated to their positions and then pick them off one by one. It would have been good to take Yavar alive for questioning.

That plan was now defunct.

Earlier that day, he'd warned Xica that it would be a good idea for her to drop out of sight for a while. She wasn't inclined to take his advice. She laughed and said she could take care of herself.

Carter wasn't going to abandon her to Tanango's tender mercies.

Reaching into his pants pocket, he pulled out a Pierre-type mini-bomb. Now was the time to act, while the ambushers were bunched together.

He thumbed down the red arming button. The tiny grenade had a five-second delay between arming and detonation.

He counted under his breath: "One one thousand, two one thousand, three one thousand—"

Leaning out from behind the forklift, he rolled the grenade across the pier toward the van.

As he ducked back under cover, he heard somebody say, "Hey, what's that?"

Somebody else yelled inarticulately.

He was silenced by the explosion of the powerful little grenade.

Carter hopped onto the forklift and hit the starter. After a blood-chilling pause, the engine fired up with a roar.

The breeze blowing in from offshore dispersed the smoke on the pier, revealing a scene of mayhem.

Yellow Shirt lay sprawled in a pool of his own blood. Beside him was his partner's mangled body.

The rifleman had dropped his weapon and held his hands over his face, screaming as he staggered blindly. He looked as if he had run into a buzz saw.

The machine gunner jumped up from behind the barrels that sheltered him. They leaked vile fluids from dozens of holes, but he was unhit.

He opened fire, squeezing off a burst of slugs that bounced off the heavy-duty steel of the lifting gear at the front of the forklift.

Pistol fire erupted from under the van, where Yavar had rolled before the grenade went off. His right arm was useless. He shot with his left hand, his bullets flying wide of the mark.

Vasquez crouched in the cab of the van, shooting with one hand while he tried to start it up.

Carter threw the forklift into gear and charged the machine gunner, who stopped shooting and started panicking as the vehicle bore down on him.

The forklift slammed into the wall of barrels, crushing the gunman beneath them.

Yavar had found his range. One of his shots breezed through Carter's hair.

The Killmaster reversed, backing away from the overturned barrels.

Vasquez had flooded his engine. He bellowed with fear-ridden rage as the forklift came toward him on a collision course.

The forklift hit the van broadside, its extended steel forks plowing through it above the rocker arm. Metal crumpled like tinfoil.

After the impact, there was an instant's resistance where neither vehicle moved.

Carter worked the gearshift and floored the gas pedal. The forklift bulled forward, shoving the van ahead of it.

Yavar crawled frantically, trying to drag himself clear. His upper body cleared the van. He still held his pistol but was too busy moving to do any shooting.

The van's right front wheel went over Yavar's midsection. His agonized scream ended in a choked gurgle.

The forklift powered the van to the edge of the pier.

Vasquez bounced around the cab. He grabbed the doorframe with both hands and started to lever himself free just as the van tilted backward.

Vasquez was thrown against the driver's side door.

Carter leaped clear as the van went over the side into the water, taking the forklift with it. He hit the ground rolling, coming up on one knee with Wilhelmina in his hand.

No one was left to oppose him.

He wasn't certain that the machine gunner was finished off for good, so he cautiously approached the jumble of barrels. The choking fumes from the spreading pool of chemical wastes were almost overpowering.

The machine gunner was dead. Pinned flat by a pile of barrels, he'd drowned in the toxic fluid.

Yavar was the worst. The crushing wheel had squeezed him in the middle like a tube of toothpaste.

The greasy gray-green water boiled with air bubbles streaming up from the sunken vehicles. Carter waited a minute, but Vasquez didn't come up.

Carter pulled the tarps from his car, hopped in, and started it up.

Wheels whirled, laying a patch of rubber as the Killmaster stomped on the gas pedal and shifted into high gear.

The car leaped forward, smashing the gates open. It hurtled down the street in a blur of speed.

Xica's apartment in Miraflores was twelve miles away.

•   •   •

Vasquez clung to a slippery piling under the pier. Seawater spilled from his nose and mouth as he gasped for breath.

When he heard Carter drive away, he swam to shore.

He knew what had to be done. There was still a chance to stop the American agent, if he could reach a phone in time.

—From NIGHT OF THE CONDOR
A New Nick Carter Spy Thriller
From Jove in November 1987

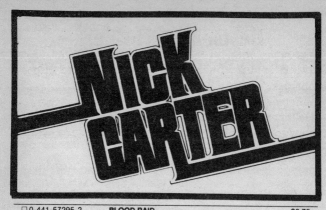

☐	0-441-57295-2	**BLOOD RAID**	$2.75
☐	0-441-57281-2	**BLOOD ULTIMATUM**	$2.50
☐	0-441-57290-1	**CROSSFIRE RED**	$2.75
☐	0-441-57282-0	**THE CYCLOPS CONSPIRACY**	$2.50
☐	0-441-14222-2	**DEATH HAND PLAY**	$2.50
☐	0-441-57292-8	**DEATH SQUAD**	$2.75
☐	0-515-09055-7	**EAST OF HELL**	$2.75
☐	0-441-21877-6	**THE EXECUTION EXCHANGE**	$2.50
☐	0-441-57294-4	**HOLY WAR**	$2.75
☐	0-441-45520-4	**THE KREMLIN KILL**	$2.50
☐	0-441-24089-5	**LAST FLIGHT TO MOSCOW**	$2.50
☐	0-441-51353-0	**THE MACAO MASSACRE**	$2.50
☐	0-441-52276-9	**THE MAYAN CONNECTION**	$2.50
☐	0-441-52510-5	**MERCENARY MOUNTAIN**	$2.50
☐	0-441-57502-1	**NIGHT OF THE WARHEADS**	$2.50
☐	0-441-58612-0	**THE NORMANDY CODE**	$2.50
☐	0-441-57289-8	**OPERATION PETROGRAD**	$2.50
☐	0-441-69180-3	**PURSUIT OF THE EAGLE**	$2.50
☐	0-441-57287-1	**SLAUGHTER DAY**	$2.50
☐	0-441-79831-4	**THE TARLOV CIPHER**	$2.50
☐	0-441-57293-6	**THE TERROR CODE**	$2.75
☐	0-441-57285-5	**TERROR TIMES TWO**	$2.50
☐	0-441-57283-9	**TUNNEL FOR TRAITORS**	$2.50
☐	0-515-09112-X	**KILLING GAMES**	$2.75
☐	0-515-09214-2	**TERMS OF VENGEANCE**	$2.75
☐	0-515-09168-5	**PRESSURE POINT**	$2.75
☐	0-515-09255-X	**NIGHT OF THE CONDOR** (on sale November '87)	$2.75

Please send the titles I've checked above. Mail orders to:

BERKLEY PUBLISHING GROUP
390 Murray Hill Pkwy., Dept. B
East Rutherford, NJ 07073

POSTAGE & HANDLING:
$1.00 for one book, $.25 for each
additional. Do not exceed $3.50.

NAME_____

ADDRESS_____

CITY_____

STATE_____ZIP_____

Please allow 6 weeks for delivery.
Prices are subject to change without notice.

BOOK TOTAL	$_____
SHIPPING & HANDLING	$_____
APPLICABLE SALES TAX (CA, NJ, NY, PA)	$_____
TOTAL AMOUNT DUE	$_____

PAYABLE IN US FUNDS.
(No cash orders accepted.)

Bestselling Thrillers —
action-packed for a great read